Love After Breakup

Healing From Past Relationships and Rebuilding Self-Love and Confidence

Adegboye Samuel

Disclaimer

The content of this book, "Love After BreakUp: Healing From Past Relationships and Rebuilding Self-Love and Confidence," is intended solely for knowledge and educational purposes. The information is based on personal insights, experiences, and general principles of relationship dynamics, personal growth, and emotional healing.

While the book offers guidance and strategies for navigating love and relationships, it is not a substitute for professional advice or therapy. The author is not a licensed therapist or mental health professional. Readers seeking therapeutic or psychological support should consult a qualified mental health professional or counselor.

The insights and suggestions presented are intended to offer support and inspiration but should not be considered definitive solutions or professional recommendations. Each individual's experiences and needs are unique, and what works for one person may not be suitable for another.

By reading this book, you acknowledge that the author, publisher, and any affiliated parties are not responsible for any outcomes, decisions, or actions based on the information provided. Use the content of this book as a tool for reflection and growth, and always seek appropriate professional guidance when dealing with personal or emotional issues.

Your well-being and personal growth are paramount, and seeking professional support can ensure you receive the best care and advice tailored to your circumstances.

Preface

Step into the world of "Love After BreakUp: Healing From Past Relationships and Rebuilding Self-Love and Confidence." As you begin your adventure through the pages of this book, I encourage you to pause and contemplate the meaning and purpose it holds.

Heartbreak is something that everyone goes through at some point in their lives. It's a shared experience that affects us all. It can be overwhelming, leaving us confused, disappointed, and lacking direction. However, during these difficult times, we often discover the potential for significant personal development. This book is a product of the realization that although heartbreak can be a profoundly challenging experience, it also has the power to bring about transformative healing and renewed hope.

"Love After Breakup" is a helpful companion for individuals embarking on the intricate path of healing and rediscovering love following complex relationships or heartbreaks. This journey allows us to come out of these experiences with a fresh perspective, a better grasp of our desires, and a willingness to embrace new opportunities.

Within these pages, you will discover a harmonious combination of personal reflections, helpful guidance, and reflective activities designed to assist you in traversing the emotional landscape of previous relationships and embracing a future abundant with love and meaningful connections. Every chapter is carefully designed to equip you with the tools and strategies to contemplate your past deeply, reconstruct your sense of self-worth, and prepare for the love ahead.

As you delve into the book, I urge you to embrace it with a receptive spirit and a readiness to reflect on yourself. Embarking on the path toward healing and discovering new love is an incredibly personal and one-of-a-kind experience for every person. Although the insights and recommendations provided here are designed to offer support and inspiration, it is essential to remember that they should be used alongside your own experiences and personal growth.

This book does not offer a universal solution, nor does it assert to possess all the answers. Instead, it serves as a companion throughout your journey—a valuable resource to help you navigate the intricate aspects of love, healing, and personal growth. I sincerely believe that "Love After BreakUp" has the potential to inspire, empower, and provide valuable insights as you navigate your journey toward a love that is both fulfilling and resilient.

Thank you for including me in your story. May this book guide you on a journey of self-discovery and empowerment, helping you overcome obstacles and open your heart to the love ahead.

Filled with a sense of warmth and optimism

Adegboye Samuel

Introduction

Understanding Heartbreak

Heartbreak is a profoundly relatable experience that knows no boundaries, reaching across cultures, ages, and backgrounds. It's an experience that nearly everyone encounters at some stage in their lives. Heartbreak is a universal experience triggered by the end of a long-term relationship, unrequited love, or the dissolution of a marriage. It profoundly affects us at our very core.

A Tale of Heartbreak That Resonates with Everyone

Picture a young woman named Sarah sitting in a warm and inviting café, gently swirling her coffee without much thought. Seated at the table, Sarah's best friend attentively listens to her as she shares the heartbreaking details of her recent breakup. Sarah's words paint a vivid picture of the weight that burdens her heart, the all-encompassing sorrow, and the relentless thoughts that consume her every waking moment. Her friend nods, showing empathy and compassion—she, too, has experienced that same pain.

Heartbreak is a universal human experience that connects us through the compassion and comprehension we offer each other. It's an indescribable feeling that has inspired countless poets, writers, and musicians throughout history, each contributing their perspective to the collective experience of love and heartbreak. Experiencing heartbreak can be a deeply emotional and raw experience. Still, it also has the power to remind us of our shared humanity and that we are never truly alone in our struggles.

The Significance of Healing Before Moving Forward

For some individuals, the anguish caused by heartbreak can be overwhelming, leading them to seek solace in the company of another person. However, recovering from heartbreak is a crucial journey that enables us to develop and gain wisdom from our encounters. Jumping into a fresh relationship without allowing yourself the necessary time to heal may result in repeating familiar patterns and carrying unresolved matters into the future.

Consider John, for example, who recently concluded a significant long-term partnership. After the breakup, he found himself adrift, lacking confidence and direction. Instead of rushing into another relationship, he paused and reflected on what went awry and what he genuinely desired in a partner. During this time of introspection, he could re-establish a connection with his inner self, rekindle his interests, and develop a more robust sense of self-value.

Healing involves more than simply letting go; it entails progressing with greater self-awareness and recognizing our requirements for a fulfilling relationship. It's a story of releasing the past and embracing fresh opportunities. It's all about turning pain into wisdom and utilizing that wisdom to shape a healthier and more satisfying future. Right after a breakup, it can be tempting to find solace in the embrace of another person. Something is captivating about starting anew, offering the hope of cleansing away the remnants of what has come before. On the other hand, rushing into a fresh relationship without giving ourselves the necessary time to heal often results in us carrying emotional burdens into the next phase of our lives. Unaddressed baggage has the potential to surface as unresolved issues, insecurities, and unhealthy patterns.

Let's delve into the tale of Lisa, a lively woman in her late twenties. Following a heart-wrenching split from her college sweetheart, Lisa was consumed by a profound sense of solitude. She swiftly embarked on a new romantic journey with Mark, a compassionate and considerate coworker, to find solace from her inner struggles. Initially, the new relationship appeared to be an ideal resolution.

Mark possessed qualities that her ex lacked—thoughtfulness, open communication, and empathy. Yet, over time, Lisa started to recognize recurring patterns.

Although Mark genuinely cared for her, Lisa grappled with insecurity and mistrust. She discovered that she was overreacting to minor issues, projecting fears from her past relationship onto Mark. Minor conflicts would ignite strong emotional reactions, and she frequently felt she was still wrestling with the remnants of her previous relationship. Lingering heartache from her breakup haunted her as she entered this fresh phase, casting a shadow over her capacity to accept and cherish Mark's affection wholeheartedly.

Lisa's story highlights the importance of finding healing before progressing forward. It is crucial to confront the unresolved pain of our past to avoid making the same errors and hindering our chances of finding happiness. Healing enables us to contemplate the events that led to the relationship's demise, acknowledge our role in it, and better understand our desires and needs in a partner.

Healing involves more than just bringing an end to a chapter; it requires comprehending the narrative that has been written and gaining wisdom from it. It's a story of recognizing our pain, mourning the absence, and ultimately discovering serenity with what transpired. It's an incredible journey of self-exploration and personal development, where we appreciate our worth and establish healthy limits to safeguard our emotional health.

Mark's relationship with Lisa started to become more and more tense. He was filled with mixed emotions, unsure and pained by Lisa's unpredictable actions, unaware of their underlying reasons. After some time, the relationship ended, leaving Lisa and Mark devastated. After their second breakup, Lisa finally decided to prioritize her healing. She decided to seek therapy, delving into her past relationship patterns, gaining insight into her attachment style, and working on developing healthier coping mechanisms.

Lisa underwent a profound transformation during this period of deep self-reflection. She embarked on a journey of self-discovery, embracing her inner power and setting new standards for her future connections. She discovered that the path to healing is not a straight line; it's a voyage filled with highs and lows, demanding patience and self-kindness. Above all, Lisa recognized that being by herself wasn't something to be afraid of—it presented a chance for her to rediscover her true self and establish a strong base for future relationships.

For those who have gone through heartbreak, it's crucial to remember that healing is essential to moving toward a happier and more satisfying future. We can embark on fresh connections with a sense of clarity and a willingness to embrace new experiences, unburdened by the ghosts of our history. Through healing, we respect ourselves and acknowledge the path we have traversed. Through our experiences, we grow in strength, wisdom, and resilience, allowing us to appreciate the profound connection that comes with love entirely.

A Healing Journey

Exploring the Concept of Healing and Personal Growth

Recovering from heartbreak is a continuous voyage, a profound and individualized experience that differs for each person. It is a journey filled with both forward strides and obstacles, instances of understanding and uncertainty. However, deep down, healing revolves around regaining our identity, rekindling our inner resilience, and nurturing our personal development.

Exploring the Concept of Healing

Picture Michael, a man in his mid-thirties, enjoying the view from his porch as the sun sets. He has experienced a difficult divorce, a marriage that ended not because of a lack of love but due to irreconcilable differences that slowly weakened the core of their relationship. At the start, Michael grappled with understanding the enormity of his defeat. His sense of self had become inseparable from his partner's, and now, in the solitude of his presence, he felt lost.

Michael's journey towards healing started by recognizing and facing his grief. He embarked on a journey of confronting the pain head-on, refusing to bury it, and embracing the entire spectrum of emotions—from anger and sadness to relief and hope. He realised that healing didn't involve erasing memories of his ex or the happy moments they had together. Instead, it meant coming to terms with the end of their story and finding solace in its resolution.

Recovery doesn't follow a straight path, and there's no fixed schedule. It's all about allowing ourselves to experience emotions, to mourn, and eventually, to move on. It's a story about showing compassion to ourselves in times of vulnerability and accepting that it's perfectly fine not to have all the answers. For individuals like Michael, finding healing can take various forms. Some may choose to seek therapy or join support groups, while others may discover it through moments of self-reflection or creative expression.

Personal Growth Through Healing

As Michael embarked on his healing journey, he started to view the experience as a chance for personal development. After his marriage ended, he began to delve into his neglected interests and passions. He decided to pursue painting, a passion that had long been neglected due to lack of time. By exploring this artistic medium, he discovered a means to convey his feelings and rediscover a fragment of his identity that had slipped away.

Exploring personal growth during healing goes beyond acquiring new skills or hobbies. It entails the journey of rediscovering our true selves beyond the confines of a relationship. It's all about grasping our values, strengths, and aspirations. Michael took the time to reflect on his role in the marriage and acknowledge the changes he needed to make for future relationships. He discovered his unique way of communicating, his patterns of attachment, and the importance of setting boundaries to safeguard his emotional well-being.

Personal growth involves embarking on a path of self-discovery and continuous self-improvement. It's a story of turning pain into purpose,utilizing the wisdom gained from previous relationships to cultivate a more submore substantial and more genuine version of oneself. Through his journey, Michael discovered the importance of embracing his independence and viewing himself as a whole person, separate from any labels or expectations tied to his relationship status. He embarked on a journey of self-discovery, charting a path towards personal and professional growth. Along the way, he crafted a life that resonated with his deepest desires and values.

The Universality of Healing and Growth
The tales of Michael, Sarah, Lisa, and Num testify to the inherent universality of the journey toward healing and personal development following a period of heartbreak. Regardless of the details, the journey typically encompasses familiar emotional territories such as grief, introspection, acceptance, and personal growth. These experiences remind us that we are not alone in our struggles. They show us that others have gone through similar journeys and that the healing process not only brings the possibility of change but also offers a profound opportunity for transformation.

Keep in mind that the path to healing is unique for each individual. Although our journeys may vary, the fundamental quest for inner peace and personal development is something we all go through as human beings.

By fully embracing this journey, we open ourselves up to the possibility of coming out of heartbreak as survivors and individuals who have developed greater strength, wisdom, and compassion. This incredible journey of healing and personal growth showcases our unwavering strength and ability to open our hearts again, armed with a profound self-awareness and a clear vision of what we truly desire in a partnership.

Establishing a Purpose for Progress

Choosing to heal and move forward after experiencing heartbreak is a crucial turning point in one's journey. It signifies a transition from dwelling on the past to embracing the potential of a fresh future. Deciding to move forward involves more than just leaving the pain behind. It requires a conscious decision to embark on a journey of self-discovery and personal growth. This choice serves as a beacon, providing guidance and optimism amidst the emotional upheaval of a broken heart.

Imagine Elena, a woman in her early forties, who had experienced the sudden and unexpected end of a relationship that had lasted for a decade. Her relationship coming to an end left her feeling utterly devastated and filled with uncertainty about what lies ahead. Weeks passed, and she couldn't escape the endless loop of reliving memories, pondering over what went awry, and doubting her value. The atmosphere was filled with darkness and uncertainty during that period, creating a sense of timelessness.

One morning, as she gazed out of her bedroom window, observing the world come alive, a change occurred within Elena. She realized that although she couldn't alter what had already happened, she possessed the power to shape her destiny. There was a serene and significant moment of understanding. With determination, she set a clear goal of healing and progress, reclaiming her life and finding her true self once again. It wasn't about hastily jumping into a fresh relationship or pressuring herself to find happiness; it was about embarking on the initial stage of a new chapter.

Establishing this intention felt akin to sowing a seed of optimism. It didn't eliminate her pain immediately, but it provided her with a reason to keep going and a clear path to follow. She started by documenting her emotions and crafting a journal chronicling her experiences. Engaging in the practice of recording her thoughts and emotions served as a therapeutic channel, enabling her to navigate through her grief and contemplate her aspirations and requirements. Expressing her purpose, she sought to mend, develop, and ultimately embrace vulnerability again.

Painting a Picture of What Lies Ahead

Elena's adventure didn't conclude with setting her intention; it was merely the start. She began to imagine the future she desired, looking past the pain of her broken heart. She pondered the desires she had longed to fulfill, yet had postponed—exploring unfamiliar destinations, acquiring fresh knowledge, and strengthening her bonds with others. She wasn't trying to escape her pain but determined to forge a fresh story for herself.

Visualizing a future where you are complete and content, regardless of the past relationship, is critical to moving forward. It's important to acknowledge that while the ties holds great importance in your life, it does not encompass your entire being. Elena found this realization to be empowering. She embarked on a series of transformations, revamping her apartment to mirror her unique style and character, enrolling in a long-awaited cooking class and re-establishing connections with long-lost friends.

These actions went beyond mere distractions; they were strides toward constructing a genuine and satisfying life. Elena's determination to progress stemmed from her conviction that she deserved happiness and love, not only from herself but also from others in due time. She discovered that establishing an intention required more than just a single action; it demanded a continuous dedication to herself. It took a lot of patience, understanding, and strength.

Embracing the Potential of Fresh Starts

Over time, Elena began to observe subtle changes within herself. She began to experience a sense of weightlessness, a newfound optimism, and a deep inner tranquility that embraced her past. She continued to experience occasional bouts of sadness and uncertainty, but they no longer consumed her entirely. With a determined spirit, she found the inner fortitude to navigate the twists and turns of her path to recovery.

Deciding to forge ahead strongly affirms valuing oneself and showing self-care. It recognizes the hurt from before while also presenting opportunities for the future. It's about dedicating oneself to personal growth, discovering new passions, and welcoming the unpredictable future with an open mind.

When faced with heartbreak, it becomes essential to set the intention to move forward to begin the healing process. It takes great bravery and serves as a powerful testament to optimism. It marks the beginning of a fresh chapter, where the past serves as a guide rather than a rule. Elena's journey is a powerful example of how setting clear intentions and having a solid spirit can lead to incredible transformation. By setting our intentions, we can discover the inner strength needed to heal, evolve, and, ultimately, experience love again.

PART 1
Reflecting On The Past

REFLECTING ON THE PAST

Reflect on the past to heal the present—by understanding the impact of your past relationships, recognizing emotional baggage, and learning from heartbreak, you pave the way for a brighter, love-filled future

Identifying the Impact of Past Relationships

Recognizing Emotional Baggage

After a relationship ends, it's typical to hold onto emotional baggage. This includes unresolved issues, fears, and insecurities from past experiences. Understanding the weight of these emotions is an essential initial stride toward healing. We gain insight into how our present selves have been influenced by past relationships and how these lasting emotions may impact our future interactions.

A man in his thirties who had recently come out of a five-year relationship. At first, relief washed over him as he thought he had escaped from all the complexities and disagreements. Yet, as he embarked on new romantic endeavors, a peculiar pattern emerged: an unexplained sense of anxiety and defensiveness. Everyday miscommunications set off strong emotions, causing him to retreat or become excessively judgemental.

One evening, following another awkward date, Alex delved deeper into his emotions. It dawned on him that a considerable amount of emotional baggage from his past relationship burdened him. His former partner frequently criticized and belittled him, resulting in feelings of inadequacy and insecurity. As time passed, Alex was plagued by an intense fear of inadequacy. This fear began to manifest as an extreme sensitivity to any perceived criticism.

Alex's life took a different direction after this recognition. He realized that the lingering emotions from his previous relationship were impacting his current actions. Gradually, he realized that his emotional burden extended beyond the breakup, encompassing unresolved issues of self-worth and trust.

The Intricacies of Carrying Emotional Burdens

Emotional baggage can sometimes go unnoticed and creep into our lives. For specific individuals, it can present itself as a fear of intimacy, where the idea of becoming emotionally close to someone once more seems daunting and frightening. To some, it may seem like a pattern of undermining potential new connections due to a lingering fear of getting hurt once more. Mistrust can often arise from past betrayals, making it challenging to have faith in the sincerity and intentions of new partners.

Consider Sarah as an example. Following the betrayal in her previous long-term relationship, she struggled to trust anyone with whom she pursued a romantic connection. Despite David's consistent and honest behavior, Sarah couldn't help but feel a lingering sense of doubt about his trustworthiness. The persistent uncertainty strained her budding relationship and hindered her ability to fully embrace the moments of happiness and intimacy she shared with David.

Sarah carried deep emotional wounds, a result of past betrayal, that left her afraid of being hurt once more. She realized that her lack of trust stemmed from her previous experiences rather than her current situation. Understanding this was the initial step in dealing with it. She embarked on a journey to delve into her emotions, realizing that although her apprehensions held weight, they may not accurately mirror her present circumstances.

Unpacking Emotional Baggage: A Path to Healing

Exploring one's emotional baggage necessitates deep self-reflection and a commitment to being truthful. Examining past relationships and identifying recurring patterns or issues affecting one's emotional state is crucial to this process. This process can be challenging, as it often uncovers difficult memories and vulnerabilities. Nevertheless, it is an essential part of the journey towards healing and progress.

Alex had to confront the pain and vulnerability he experienced during his previous relationship to address his emotional baggage. He began documenting his experiences, delving into the effects of his ex-partner's criticisms on his self-esteem. Additionally, he pursued therapy to focus on rebuilding his sense of self-worth and cultivating more effective coping mechanisms.

Just like that, Sarah took the initiative to address her trust issues by having an honest conversation with David about her fears and past experiences. She consciously tried to stay in the present moment and avoid allowing past betrayals to influence her judgment. Through this process, she slowly regained her trust and truly embraced her relationship with David.

Progressing with Consciousness

Understanding and dealing with emotional baggage involves taking responsibility for our own emotions and experiences without blaming ourselves or others for what has happened in the past. It revolves around developing a sense of self-awareness and embracing personal accountability for one's emotional well-being. By recognizing the lasting impact of previous relationships, we can initiate the healing process and safeguard ourselves against obstacles that may hinder our future contentment.

Alex's realization of his emotional baggage enabled him to approach new relationships with a more positive and balanced perspective. He developed a heightened sense of his triggers and improved his ability to express his needs and set boundaries. The realization of one's own identity served as a solid basis for fostering deeper, genuine relationships.

Sarah's recognition of her trust issues allowed her to cultivate a more profound and sincere connection with David. She realized that trust is not something that comes easily but rather a conscious decision and ongoing effort. It demands both effort and vulnerability. Through facing her fears head-on, she embraced the potential for love and meaningful connections, leaving behind the haunting memories of her past.

Understanding and acknowledging the weight of past experiences is a brave and essential part of finding inner peace and moving forward. It provides insight into how our past experiences influence our present circumstances and gives us the ability to shape our future. By embracing this newfound understanding, we can cultivate stronger, more enriching connections free from the lingering shadows of our history.

Exploring Patterns and Triggers

As we heal from previous relationships, we must grasp the recurring patterns and triggers that have surfaced throughout our journey. Patterns in our behavior, choice of partners, or emotional responses can provide valuable insights into our underlying needs, fears, and unresolved issues. By acknowledging and comprehending these components, we can liberate ourselves from detrimental patterns and approach forthcoming relationships with heightened self-awareness and purpose.

Exploring Patterns

Lisa, a woman in her late twenties, had experienced a string of relationships that all seemed to follow a familiar pattern. Every time, she would become completely infatuated, pour her heart into meeting her partner's needs, and eventually end up feeling ignored and unsatisfied. After experiencing multiple disappointments, Lisa started recognizing a recurring theme: she consistently found herself in relationships with individuals who were not emotionally accessible or ready to commit fully.

Coming to this realization was a difficult journey. Lisa was faced with the daunting task of confronting some uncomfortable truths about herself and the choices she had made. She remembered her childhood when she frequently longed to gain love and approval from her distant parents. Through this experience, she developed a deep-seated belief that love required effort and that her needs were always on the back burner. Throughout her adult life, she was naturally drawn to partners who reflected this pattern, unknowingly continuing a cycle of emotional lack.

Lisa's recognition of this pattern marked a significant turning point. She came to realize that her recurring experiences were not just random occurrences but rather connected to unresolved issues from her past. With this newfound awareness, she began to make different choices, gravitating toward partners who appreciated emotional intimacy and reciprocity.

Recognizing what sets off specific reactions

In addition to recognizing patterns, it is crucial to fully identify triggers to comprehend the effects of previous relationships. Triggers are intense emotional reactions that may seem disproportionate to the present circumstances, often stemming from past traumas or unresolved emotions. These reactions can appear as strong responses to certain words, actions, or situations. They might seem illogical or exaggerated to others, but hold great significance for the individual going through them.

Consider David, a man who endured a turbulent relationship characterized by manipulation and emotional abuse. Despite the breakup, David discovered he still had intense emotional responses to specific circumstances. When his new partner, Emma, had to cancel a date because of a work emergency, David couldn't help but feel a wave of anger and betrayal, even though he understood her reasons.

After some thought, David realized that his response was influenced by his previous relationship, in which his ex-partner would often cancel plans to exert control and manipulate him at the last minute. He was left feeling powerless and insecure due to these experiences. Emma's actions, though innocent, brought back those old wounds.

Through the discovery of this trigger, David was able to gain a deeper understanding of his emotional landscape. He realized that his solid emotional response had more to do with the lasting hurt from his past relationship rather than Emma's actions. With this newfound understanding, he could have honest conversations with Emma, addressing his emotions and actively working towards establishing trust and stability in their relationship.

A Story of Breaking Free

Gaining insight into patterns and triggers goes beyond mere recognition; it involves liberating oneself from one's grasp. Lisa consciously decided to pursue relationships with individuals who consistently demonstrated care and emotional availability. It also required establishing limits and giving importance to her needs, which she had overlooked previously.

David had to confront his trust issues and improve his self-esteem to break the cycle. He sought the guidance of a therapist to navigate the emotional aftermath of his previous relationship and cultivate more effective ways of dealing with his experiences. In addition, he incorporated mindfulness into his routine to better control his emotional responses and remain centered in the present moment.

Lisa and David discovered that to break these patterns and handle triggers, they had to make a deliberate effort and be open to facing uncomfortable emotions. Through a gradual process and unwavering determination, they started noticing shifts in their actions and emotional reactions. They began approaching relationships with a newfound sense of clarity, confidence, and a heightened self-awareness.

A Tale of Uncovering One's True Identity

Understanding patterns and triggers is a personal journey of self-discovery. It takes deep self-reflection and a readiness to confront challenging realities about oneself. Yet, it also explores one's inner depths and the pursuit of liberation from emotional constraints. Understanding the root causes of our actions and responses allows us to embark on a healing journey and cultivate a more nourishing and satisfying present.

This journey had a profound impact on Lisa and David. They became aware of their tendency to repeat familiar behaviors and consciously tried to change their course of action. They developed a heightened sensitivity to their emotional triggers and learned to handle them with empathy and insight. Above all, they realized they could alter their stories and cultivate connections aligned with their genuine aspirations and principles.

As we delve into our patterns and triggers, we unlock the pathway to profound healing and personal development. We gain the tools to escape from negative patterns and build a life and connections that truly reflect who we are at our core. Although filled with obstacles, this adventure is crucial to progress and discovering love after our relationship.

Lessons Gained from Heartbreak

Acquiring Insight and Wisdom

Experiencing heartbreak can be a painful experience, but it can also be an opportunity for personal growth and self-discovery. By going through the journey of navigating emotional turmoil and loss, we acquire valuable insights into ourselves and our relationships. These lessons, born from the depths of pain, serve as beacons of wisdom illuminating our path forward. Grasping the insights gained from heartbreak empowers us to convert our experiences into chances for personal development and greater comprehension.

Uncovering the Depths of Knowledge

Ethan, a man in his mid-thirties, was trapped in a cycle of making the same mistakes—selecting partners who didn't align with his values and aspirations and attempting to change himself to fit into the relationship. Following his latest breakup, Ethan experienced a deep feeling of disappointment. He paused and contemplated his previous relationships, aiming to comprehend the reasons for their failures. As Ethan reflected on his past, he realized that he often overlooked warning signs in the early stages of his relationships. He would disregard significant disparities in values and lifestyle, persuading himself that love could overcome any divide. Unfortunately, this frequently resulted in a slow deterioration of his identity as he made concessions on matters that held significance for him. Ethan's consistent tendency to prioritize the needs of others over his well-being ultimately left him with a sense of dissatisfaction and bitterness.

Ethan experienced a significant shift in his perspective. He realized that his heartbreaks were more than just setbacks; they were chances to gain insight into his desires and limitations. He started to recognize the significance of being truthful with himself and his partners regarding his desires in a relationship. Through this realization, he understood that genuine compatibility extends beyond physical attraction. It encompasses the harmonization of fundamental beliefs and aspirations for the future.

Embracing the Lessons

Imagine Maya, a woman in her late twenties, who experienced the heart-wrenching aftermath of a breakup when she uncovered her partner's betrayal. The betrayal completely crushed her, and she began to doubt her judgment. Maya was grappling with a whirlwind of emotions, burdened by a sense of responsibility and a lack of trust. But as time passed, she started to think back on the relationship and the clues she had overlooked.

Maya realized that she had frequently disregarded her intuition, dismissing feelings of unease or discomfort. She realized that she tended to prioritize her partner's happiness at the expense of her well-being, frequently disregarding her own needs and emotions to avoid potential conflicts. Through deep reflection, Maya came to a significant realization: she must have faith in her instincts and prioritize her emotional well-being.

Armed with this newfound understanding, Maya began establishing firmer boundaries in her relationships. She discovered the importance of trusting her instincts and responding when something seemed amiss. Through a challenging experience, she gained the strength to make better decisions and focus on her emotional well-being.

Turning Pain into Personal Growth

Ethan and Maya demonstrate how heartbreak can serve as a transformative force, propelling individuals toward personal development. By going through various experiences, they were able to gain valuable insights into their patterns, needs, and boundaries. They discovered that the anguish of a broken heart, although complex, can bring about profound change. It offers a chance to ponder our relationship desires and explore ways to foster healthier, more satisfying connections.

Ethan's lesson revolved around the importance of being genuine and deeply understanding oneself. He realized that he needed to stay authentic and find like-minded individuals who shared his beliefs and aspirations for the future. Maya learned an important lesson about trusting herself and establishing boundaries. She recognized the significance of respecting her emotions and safeguarding her emotional welfare.

A Glimpse into the Future

Heartbreak has a way of imparting wisdom that reaches far beyond just romantic relationships. Its impact can be felt in every aspect of our lives. It shows us the power of bouncing back, being kind to ourselves, and embracing our true selves. By adopting these teachings, we are better prepared to face future obstacles with poise and understanding.

Ethan and Maya emerged from their experiences with a newfound self-awareness and a stronger sense of purpose in their lives and relationships. They discovered that the experience of heartbreak can be both painful and enlightening. It reveals the truth and compels us to face complex realities, ultimately guiding us toward a deeper understanding of ourselves and inner resilience.

As we contemplate our encounters with heartbreak, we can also discover valuable insights. By acquiring understanding and knowledge, we can turn our suffering into a wellspring of strength. We gain a deeper understanding of navigating future relationships with greater mindfulness, empathy, and purpose. Through this journey, heartbreak transforms from a mere conclusion into a new chapter—an invitation to evolve, gain wisdom, and ultimately discover an authentic and satisfying love.

Identifying Warning Signs and Positive Indicators

After experiencing heartbreak, individuals often deeply introspect, contemplating the factors that led to their pain and considering how to approach future relationships with greater wisdom. Through self-reflection, one can better understand the significance of identifying warning signs and positive indicators in a relationship. Gaining a deeper understanding of these signals can empower individuals to make wiser choices and cultivate meaningful connections that resonate with their values and desires.

Identifying Red Flags

Sophia, a woman in her early thirties, had recently emerged from a turbulent relationship. Throughout their time together, she frequently experienced a sense of unease and self-doubt, even though she struggled to identify the root cause of these emotions. Following the breakup, she dedicated herself to introspection, aiming to gain insight into the root causes of the relationship's demise. Sophia realized she had overlooked multiple warning signs, convincing herself that things would improve over time.

It was pretty concerning to see how her ex-partner consistently undermined her emotions. Whenever Sophia shared her concerns or feelings, he would brush them off as exaggerated or belittle her experiences. She was left with a sense of being ignored and dismissed. In addition, he often found fault with her choices and decisions, subtly eroding her self-assurance. These actions, although not explicitly abusive, gradually undermined her self-esteem and caused her to question her perceptions.

There was cause for concern when he showed hesitancy in being transparent. Whenever conflicts arose, he would become unresponsive or defensive, hindering the constructive resolution of issues. The absence of effective communication led to a recurring pattern of unresolved tensions, leaving Sophia frustrated and isolated.

After carefully considering these warning signs, Sophia realized that her former partner's actions revealed underlying problems—specifically, emotional immaturity and a noticeable absence of empathy. She realized that disregarding these indications had played a part in her long-lasting discontentment and emotional anguish. She felt empowered by this realization, which led her to establish more precise boundaries in future relationships and prioritize partners who genuinely respected and valued her emotions.

Recognizing Green Flags

However, it is just as crucial to acknowledge a partner's positive traits and behaviors, which can be seen as green flags. These signs indicate that an individual can sustain a positive and nurturing relationship. Reflecting on his past relationship, Mark, a man in his late twenties who had also gone through a painful breakup, gained valuable insights into what he truly valued in a partner.

Mark had been in a relationship with a woman who, despite the eventual end, had shown several positive signs that he grew to value greatly. She always stood by his side, offering unwavering support for his dreams and aspirations. Her encouragement was genuine, free from any hint of envy or bitterness. She was always forthcoming and sincere, even during challenging discussions. Their openness allowed them to approach challenges and misunderstandings with empathy and comprehension.

One positive aspect was her willingness to accept accountability for her actions. During times of disagreement, she demonstrated a willingness to admit her errors and make efforts to resolve them. Their maturity and accountability laid the groundwork for a relationship built on mutual respect and trust.

Despite their eventual breakup caused by divergent life goals, Mark recognized the importance of these positive qualities in a partner. He understood that a relationship built on support, open communication, and mutual respect was much more satisfying and long-lasting.

Discovering the Power of Intuition

The experiences of both Sophia and Mark highlight the significance of relying on one's instincts when identifying warning signs and positive indicators. Sophia's sense of unease and discomfort hinted at an underlying issue, even though she struggled to explain it. Mark's recognition of his former partner's positive qualities underscored the importance of a supportive and considerate relationship.

Through introspection, both individuals gained a profound insight into their desires and requirements within a relationship. It became clear to them that sure signs can indicate potential issues, evoking a sense of unease, while other signs can bring comfort and satisfaction. Having faith in these instinctive reactions can serve as a valuable compass when assessing a relationship's well-being and future prospects.

Progressing with Consciousness

As Sophia and Mark continued their journey, they carried with them the valuable insights gained from identifying warning signs and positive indicators. Sophia became more attentive to how potential partners treated her and others, while Mark actively sought partners who exhibited the positive qualities he valued. They both recognized that these lessons focused on developing a heightened understanding of their needs and limits rather than simply following a set of rules.

Their stories emphasize that identifying warning signs and positive indicators is continuous. It requires being aware of one's emotions, being truthful with oneself about any worries, and acknowledging the positive qualities that contribute to a strong relationship. Through this approach, people can confidently navigate the intricacies of dating and relationships, ultimately guiding them toward more meaningful and genuine connections.

Throughout this narrative of introspection and personal growth, identifying warning signs and positive indicators becomes essential. It enables individuals to make choices that align with their values and well-being, allowing them to steer clear of harmful dynamics and cultivate relationships based on mutual respect and sincere affection. Through the lessons learned from previous heartaches, this invaluable wisdom illuminates the way to discovering and cultivating love beyond our past.

Discovering the Power of Forgiveness

Forgiving Yourself and Your Ex

Embarking on the path of healing from previous relationships can lead us to a pivotal and demanding crossroads: forgiveness. Forgiveness, often misconstrued as accepting harmful behavior, is about letting go of anger, resentment, and regret. It's a compassionate gesture towards oneself and others, enabling us to progress unburdened by the past. This process encompasses two crucial elements: granting ourselves forgiveness for our mistakes and imperfections and extending forgiveness to our former partners for theirs.

Forgiving Yourself

Emma, a woman in her early forties, had been grappling with feelings of guilt and self-blame following the dissolution of her marriage. She frequently relived instances where she wished she had made different choices—communicated her desires more effectively, asserted herself with greater confidence, or encouraged her former spouse's aspirations. Haunted by these regrets, she found it challenging to move forward and began questioning her capacity for a healthy future relationship.

Emma pondered her marriage and realized she had been too hard on herself. She admitted to her errors and acknowledged that she had given her utmost effort given the circumstances. She had experienced a profound love and had dedicated herself entirely. However, she also understood that their marriage's success did not rest solely on her shoulders. The end of their relationship was not a reflection of her value but a result of a partnership that no longer benefited both individuals.

Emma's path to self-forgiveness required a change in how she saw things. She started to view herself as someone who had evolved and gained wisdom from her life encounters rather than someone who had faced setbacks. She fully embraced the concept that making mistakes is an inherent aspect of life and that every experience, even the painful ones, contributes to personal growth. With this newfound understanding, she could release the burden of self-blame and extend the same kindness to herself that she so readily gave to others.

Forgiving your Ex

Like forgiving an ex-partner, the process can be equally challenging but crucial for genuine healing. Forgiveness is not about making excuses for harmful behavior or erasing the pain it caused. Instead, it involves freeing ourselves from the grip of anger and resentment. It's a powerful experience that sets us free emotionally, enabling us to regain our inner peace and move forward with a renewed sense of lightness.

James, a man in his late twenties, found forgiving his ex-girlfriend challenging and emotionally taxing. Their relationship came to an abrupt end when she betrayed his trust, leaving him feeling devastated and deeply wounded. James clung to his anger for an extended period, constantly reliving the betrayal and nurturing a feeling of unfairness. Gradually, his growing resentment started seeping into various aspects of his life, casting a shadow over his mood and making it harder for him to trust others.

Once upon a time, James realized that clinging onto his anger was only prolonging his suffering. Instead of seeking revenge or seeking justice, he found himself trapped in a never-ending cycle of negativity. He chose to embark on the journey of forgiveness, not out of concern for her well-being but for his personal growth. He had to face the pain and sense of betrayal, allowing himself to mourn and eventually releasing the anger.

James discovered that forgiveness is an ongoing decision rather than a one-time event. Some days, the lingering pain resurfaced, forcing him to reaffirm his dedication to moving forward. He also recognized that forgiving her didn't imply endorsing her actions or pretending everything was fine. Releasing the emotional baggage holding him back and refusing to let the past dictate his present and future was a significant step for him.

Liberation Through Forgiveness

Emma and James experienced a deep sense of liberation through forgiveness. Emma's perspective shifted, freeing her from the weight of past mistakes. Now, she could embrace future relationships with a newfound clarity and a stronger sense of who she is and what she wants. She discovered the power of following her intuition, establishing healthier limits, and finding solace in self-forgiveness for previous missteps. James, however, experienced a sense of relief as he let go of his anger and pain. He discovered a newfound openness to unfamiliar adventures and connections, unburdened by the resentment of his previous experiences.

They realized that forgiveness is not about reconciling or erasing memories; it's about taking control of one's emotions and overall happiness. It's a story of embracing peace instead of holding onto bitterness and choosing love over resentment. Releasing and moving on is essential to the healing process, enabling us to progress with clarity and elegance.

Progressing with Forgiveness

Looking back on our past relationships, we must understand the significance of forgiving ourselves and our ex-partners as we move forward. It's a journey that demands understanding and empathy for us and those around us. Through forgiveness, we liberate ourselves from the burdens of past pain and unlock the potential for fresh opportunities. We discover the art of embracing future relationships with a heart that is open and free from the weight of past experiences.

By embracing forgiveness, we extend a generous gesture to others and demonstrate a deep sense of self-care and honor. We can celebrate our personal stories, recognize our progress, and welcome what lies ahead with positivity and anticipation. For Emma, James, and everyone involved, the journey towards healing and discovering love after our experiences starts with the transformative strength of forgiveness.

The Importance of Finding Closure and Embracing Acceptance

When a relationship ends, a complex mix of emotions tends to arise. There's often a sense of bewilderment, sorrow, frustration, and occasionally even a feeling of liberation. Coming to terms with the end of a relationship can be incredibly difficult, especially when it comes to finding closure and accepting that it's truly over. Coming to terms with our experiences and finding inner tranquility does not always require a specific conversation or a conclusive resolution. It entails embracing a state of emotional harmony, where we can acknowledge what transpired, gain wisdom from it, and release it from our grasp. Acceptance is a calm recognition that, even though there may have been pain and disappointment, the relationship has fulfilled its role and it is now time to progress.

Seeking Resolution

Let's delve into the tale of Hannah, who found herself in a long-term relationship that ended abruptly. Months passed since the breakup, leaving her adrift and overwhelmed by unanswered inquiries. What led to the downfall? Is there any way she could have approached the situation differently? Due to these persistent doubts, Hannah struggled to find closure and move forward in her life.

Hannah realized that she clung to the hope of her ex-partner returning and offering an explanation, which would bring her the much-needed clarity she yearned for. Yet, as time passed, it became evident that this reconciliation was not meant to be. Hannah realized that holding out for resolution from her former partner only extended her suffering. She had to discover it deep within her.

She started by contemplating the connection, its conclusion, and the entire voyage. Hannah reflected on their happy moments and deep connection, yet she also confronted the harsh truth of the problems that ultimately caused their separation. She diligently recorded her thoughts and emotions, finding solace in this therapeutic practice that aided her in navigating her feelings and gaining a more lucid understanding. Through introspection, she clarified the reasons behind the end of the relationship and realized that she and her ex had drifted apart.

Hannah also participated in a meaningful gesture of conclusion. She collected keepsakes from their shared experiences—pictures, notes, and presents—and chose to release them. Instead of discarding them, she placed them in a box and stored them away, out of view. This act was not focused on eliminating the past but on recognizing it and making room for fresh memories and experiences.

Hannah discovered a sense of closure by following these steps. She came to terms with the fact that she might never find all the answers she sought, but she realized she didn't require them to progress. Embracing the unknown set her free, enabling her to release the burden of her emotions.

Embracing Acceptance

Michael, a man in his mid-thirties, faced the daunting task of not only seeking closure but also coming to terms with the fact that the future he had once imagined with his former partner was now out of reach. They had envisioned a future filled with love and commitment—a life built on marriage, raising children, and creating a home together. When the relationship ended, it felt as though all those hopes and aspirations had been completely crushed.

Michael grappled with the concept of acceptance. He believed that embracing the end of the relationship signified relinquishing his aspirations and acknowledging defeat. As he processed his emotions, he started to view acceptance as a brave recognition of the truth rather than a form of giving up. The story revolves around confronting the situation's reality and deciding to progress instead of remaining trapped in a cycle of remorse and hypotheticals.

Michael's acceptance was a slow and gradual process. He began by centering his attention on the present moment, choosing not to linger on the past or fret about what lies ahead. He embraced new hobbies, rekindled old friendships, and delved into his passions. Engaging in these activities allowed him to reconnect with who he was and separate from the relationship. It was a powerful reminder that there was so much more to life than he had initially planned.

Michael understood the importance of being kind to himself, acknowledging that he was expected to feel sadness over the end of the relationship and his future dreams. He embraced the emotions of sorrow and disappointment yet remained determined to discover happiness through new adventures. He understood that acceptance was not something that happened just once but rather a continuous journey of finding peace with the past and embracing the potential of the future.

The Transformative Influence of Finding Closure and Embracing Acceptance

Hannah and Michael embarked on a deeply personal and unique journey towards closure and acceptance. They had to face their emotions head-on, deeply contemplate their experiences, and ultimately find acceptance after their relationships. By finding closure and embracing acceptance, they could let go of the past's grip on their emotions and thoughts, making room for fresh starts.

These experiences showcase the profound impact that closure and acceptance can have. It's important to remember that moving on from past relationships doesn't mean forgetting or downplaying their significance. Instead, it's about acknowledging the value of those experiences and the personal growth they brought. By finding closure and embracing acceptance, individuals can release any lingering pain and resentment that may hold them back. This allows them to open themselves to new opportunities for love and happiness.

Progressing Ahead

As we look back on our previous relationships, finding closure and embracing acceptance provide a way to heal. They remind us that although we cannot alter the past, we can mold our current circumstances and future. Through the process of finding closure, we recognize and appreciate our past experiences while also releasing ourselves from the burden of lingering emotions.

As we progress, we hold onto the wisdom gained, the progress made, and the optimism for what lies ahead. Coming to terms with our past and finding peace does not mean forgetting it but rather incorporating it into our personal story to strengthen us. We can fully embrace the journey of healing and self-discovery, feeling confident in our capacity to love once more and find happiness in fresh starts.

PART 2
Rebuilding Self-Love And Confidence

REBUILDING SELF-LOVE AND CONFIDENCE

Rediscover your worth and reignite your passions—by rebuilding self-love, overcoming negative self-talk, and embracing your unique journey, you empower yourself to attract the love and life you truly deserve

Rediscovering Your Self-Worth

Emphasizing Your Worth and Deservingness

Following the conclusion of a meaningful relationship, numerous individuals experience a struggle with a decreased sense of self-esteem. When a partnership ends, it can often lead to self-doubt and questions about one's worthiness of love and happiness. Embarking on the path to reclaiming one's sense of value is crucial in constructing a well-rounded and satisfying existence. This journey is about rediscovering one's worth and embracing the idea that every person deserves love, respect, and happiness, regardless of their past.

Discovering Your Worth

Following a heart-wrenching split, Sarah, a woman in her late twenties, found herself adrift and lacking confidence. Their relationship had been filled with ups and downs, characterized by her ex-partner's ongoing criticism and emotional manipulation. As time passed, these unfortunate encounters gradually wore away at Sarah's sense of self-worth, leaving her with feelings of inadequacy and unworthiness. She started to accept her ex's hurtful remarks about her, internalizing them as undeniable facts.

After the breakup, Sarah found it difficult to recognize her value. She had uncertainties about her abilities and insecurities about her attractiveness, and she wondered if she would ever come across someone who genuinely loved and valued her. These feelings of uncertainty were intensified by the apprehension of solitude and the expectations from society to be in a partnership.

Sarah embarked on a journey to rediscover her worth, taking small yet meaningful strides along the way. She began by separating herself from the negative story that her ex had forced upon her. She reached out to her loved ones for help, and they reassured her by highlighting her strengths and positive attributes. Her affirmations provided a much-needed antidote to the pessimistic thoughts that plagued her mind.

Sarah found solace in participating in activities that brought her immense happiness and a feeling of fulfillment. She rediscovered past hobbies set aside during the relationship and ventured into uncharted territories of new interests. She enrolled in a nearby art class and uncovered a deep love for painting. Sarah found solace in creating art, as it allowed her to express herself freely and served as a therapeutic release for her emotions.

As Sarah went through these experiences, she rediscovered her true self. She realized that her value was not determined by her previous romantic involvement or the viewpoints of her former partner. Her worth came from within, stemming from her distinct qualities, abilities, and compassion towards others. As she discovered this, she felt a newfound sense of freedom, which allowed her to regain her confidence and self-worth.

Having confidence in your worthiness

Recognizing one's value is often just the beginning. The next important step is to fully believe that one deserves all the good things in life, such as love, happiness, and respect. For individuals who have gone through unhealthy or abusive relationships, this belief can be challenging to overcome. In such relationships, they may have been constantly made to feel unworthy or undeserving.

Alex, a man in his early thirties, had endured a long and challenging relationship where his needs were consistently ignored, and his emotions were consistently invalidated. His former partner frequently made him feel like he was being overly demanding or irrational. As time passed, Alex absorbed these messages and started questioning whether he deserved kindness and consideration from others.

Following their split, Alex struggled to express his needs and desires in romantic situations and all aspects of their life. He frequently accepted less than he deserved, afraid that he would be perceived as demanding or unappreciative if he requested more. His perspective trapped him in constant discontent, hindering him from embracing potential avenues that could have brought him happiness and satisfaction.

Alex's perspective shifted after a meaningful discussion with a mentor who urged him to contemplate his desires for life and relationships deeply. The mentor asked, "Do you think you deserve happiness?" This question compelled Alex to face his inner insecurities and the self-imposed limitations he had embraced.

Alex started questioning these beliefs after reflecting on them and showing them kindness. He realized that everyone, including himself, deserves to be treated with respect and compassion. He began incorporating self-affirmations into his daily routine, consistently reminding himself of his inherent worthiness of love and happiness. In his interactions with others, he made it clear that he had certain boundaries, standing up for himself and not tolerating mistreatment.

As Alex fully embraced his worthiness, he couldn't help but notice a significant change in his relationships and the opportunities that came his way. He drew in individuals who regarded him with respect and gratitude, and he experienced a boost in confidence to pursue his passions. He realized that he deserved good things, which motivated him to actively seek experiences that resonated with his values and brought him immense joy.

The Journey of Rediscovery

Recognizing and embracing one's worth and deservingness is a continuous process. Consistently nurturing a positive self-image and rejecting negative beliefs imposed by others or internalized through past experiences is essential to this process. This story revolves around embracing one's inherent worth and acknowledging that everyone deserves love, respect, and happiness.

This journey had a profound impact on Sarah and Alex. They uncovered their inner strengths, reignited their passions, and experienced the pure happiness of embracing their authentic selves. They discovered the importance of establishing limits, prioritizing their well-being, and entering into relationships with strong self-respect and confidence. Above all, they understood that their value did not depend on others' approval but was an inherent aspect of their being.

Embracing the Future with Assurance

As we journey towards healing and personal growth, we must constantly remind ourselves of our worth and that we deserve a healthy and fulfilling life. It allows us to make decisions that align with our authentic selves, foster deep connections, and confidently chase our aspirations.

By fully embracing our value, we can heal from previous hurts and establish a solid groundwork for a future abundant with love, happiness, and a deep sense of self-worth. This incredible journey showcases the unwavering strength of the human soul and the profound impact of embracing oneself with love.

Conquering the Power of Negative Self-Talk

Self-critical thoughts can be a harmful internal dialogue that chips away at one's self-esteem and confidence, especially in the aftermath of a breakup or a challenging relationship. These thoughts can be harsh and make you question yourself, amplifying feelings of not being good enough or deserving. Conquering this harmful cycle is essential to rebuilding a positive relationship with oneself and finding one's actual value.

The Voice of the Inner Critic

Consider the story of Lisa, who, following the conclusion of a significant relationship, discovered herself trapped in a pattern of detrimental self-dialogue. Her relationship had come to a bitter end, as her partner had taken the opportunity to highlight what they saw as her flaws and shortcomings. Long after the relationship ended, these negative comments continued to haunt her thoughts, becoming a constant presence in her inner thoughts.

Lisa constantly battled with her insecurities and doubts. The critical voice inside her head never failed to remind her of her perceived shortcomings and mistakes. It seemed there was no escape from the barrage of negative thoughts, which only served to chip away at her self-assurance.

Lisa's constant negative self-talk had become deeply rooted within her, leaving little room for doubt or questioning. She embraced these thoughts as undeniable facts, shaping her choices and interactions with those around her. For example, she refrained from pursuing a promotion at work, convinced she lacked the ability or worthiness to succeed. She always felt a sense of unease and doubt in social settings, confident that those around her were silently scrutinizing her every move.

Understanding and Confronting Unhelpful Thoughts

One crucial aspect of conquering negative self-talk is being aware of its occurrence and acknowledging its presence. During a therapy session, Lisa had a realization. Her therapist guided her in recognizing the negative patterns in her thinking. They talked about how these thoughts might not accurately represent her abilities and values.

After gaining this newfound understanding, Lisa embarked on a journey of practicing mindfulness. She began to carefully observe her thoughts, refraining from immediately accepting them as absolute truths. Upon recognizing negative self-talk, she took a moment to pause and reflect on the validity of these thoughts. She pondered, questioning the validity of the situation and considering how she would advise a friend in a similar predicament.

Through this process of questioning, Lisa was able to distance herself from her inner critic and gain a more objective perspective on her thoughts. She realised that a lot of her negative thoughts about herself stemmed from past events and anxieties rather than what was happening in the present. Take, for instance, the notion that she was constantly unsuccessful. This perception was called into question by her many accomplishments, ranging from significant milestones to minor victories.

Transforming Negative Self-Talk into Empowering Affirmations

After becoming conscious of her negative self-talk, Lisa tried to replace these detrimental thoughts with positive affirmations. The focus here was not on disregarding challenges or painting a rosy picture of reality but rather on cultivating a compassionate and encouraging inner dialogue. She started acknowledging her strengths, achievements, and values.

Lisa would begin her day each morning by gazing into the mirror and reciting uplifting statements. She would declare, "I possess the ability and merit to achieve success," "I am deserving of love and admiration," and "I am sufficient, exactly as I am." These affirmations seemed challenging for her to accept, but gradually, they began to take root and transform her perspective.

Lisa diligently maintained a journal to record her daily achievements and uplifting moments. Through this practice, she could shift her attention toward the positive aspects of her life and acknowledge the strides she had made. She started constructing a new story about herself through consistently reinforcing positive thoughts - an empowering and affirming story.

The Importance of Self-Compassion

Developing self-compassion is a crucial aspect of conquering negative self-talk. Lisa understood the importance of being kind to herself during challenging moments and acknowledging that nobody is perfect and mistakes are inevitable. Instead of being overly critical of herself for what she saw as failures, she discovered how to approach these moments with empathy and compassion.

When Lisa felt disappointed about not getting the job she applied for, instead of letting it bring her down, she remembered that rejection is a normal part of life and doesn't define her value. Despite feeling disappointed, she recognized her attempt's value and admired her bravery in submitting her application. Her ability to show compassion enabled her to recover with strength and persevere in pursuing her aspirations.

Changing the Inner Conversation

Lisa's path to conquering her inner critic was far from straightforward or effortless. She encountered obstacles and experienced uncertainty along the way, but through perseverance and dedication, she slowly changed the way she spoke to herself. She discovered the power of identifying and questioning negative thoughts, replacing them with uplifting affirmations, and treating herself with kindness and understanding.

Lisa's life took a remarkable turn, allowing her to chase after her aspirations and embrace her true self. She successfully landed a new job that perfectly matched her interests, explored new hobbies, and formed more meaningful connections. Her transformation was evident in how she presented herself and engaged with the world.

The Strength of Optimistic Self-Dialogue

Conquering the habit of negative self-talk can be a transformative journey toward reclaiming one's self-esteem and cultivating a stronger sense of confidence. It takes time, dedication, and a willingness to improve oneself. As Lisa's story demonstrates, altering how we speak to ourselves can profoundly affect our general well-being and perspective on life.

Through fostering a constructive and empathetic inner narrative, we can acknowledge our worth, embrace our abilities, and confront life's obstacles with resilience and a positive outlook. This shift brings about a positive change in our relationship with ourselves and allows for healthier and more loving connections with others. Embarking on the path of self-love and confidence is a continuous process, where every step brings us closer to embracing our authentic selves and recognizing our worth.

Rediscovering Your Passions and Interests

Embracing the Beauty of Solitude

After a breakup or the end of a relationship, it's common to experience uncertainty and solitude. Going from being in a relationship to being alone can be overwhelming, with a range of emotions, such as sadness, fear, and uncertainty. Nevertheless, this period presents a chance for personal growth, as one can explore one's true self, reignite past interests, and embrace unattached happiness.

Embracing the Joy of Being Single

Following her divorce, Maria discovered herself in a life that was almost unrecognizable to her. She had been married for over ten years, during which her sense of self became closely tied to her responsibilities as a spouse and parent. After the marriage ended, Maria grappled with her identity beyond the confines of those roles. During the first few months, she faced numerous challenges and experienced a sense of being lost, struggling with overwhelming emotions of grief and a void inside.

As time passed, Maria started to view her newfound singleness as an opportunity for self-expression and personal growth. She dedicated this period to rediscovering the passions and pastimes she had neglected while being married. Maria had always been fond of painting, a passion she had set aside because of the responsibilities of family life. Now, she discovered a sense of peace and happiness as she returned to the easel.

With every stroke of the brush, she felt as though she was embarking on a journey of self-discovery. She began her artistic journey by creating serene landscapes, gradually venturing into abstract expression. She found the process to be genuinely freeing, enabling her to convey previously indescribable emotions and re-establish a connection with a forgotten aspect of herself. Her living room quickly transformed into an art studio, brimming with canvases, paints, and the lively commotion of creativity.

Embarking on a Journey of Discovery

As Maria embraced her single status, she discovered a world of new interests waiting to be explored while also rediscovering old passions. She embraced yoga, finding it to be a transformative practice that improved her physical well-being and brought about a sense of mental clarity and inner peace. Engaging in mindfulness and meditation became a regular part of her routine, providing her with stability and support as she faced the emotional challenges following her divorce.

Maria decided to finally pursue her long-time dream of taking a cooking class, which had always been on her mind but had been put on hold due to lack of time. She found joy in exploring various cuisines, realizing the calming effect of cooking, and enjoying the company of friends while sharing her creations. Her kitchen transformed into a hub of culinary exploration, and she frequently extended invitations to friends for dinner, creating an inviting atmosphere in her home with joyous laughter and delectable cuisine.

These activities held a more profound meaning beyond mere hobbies - they served as a means of exploring oneself and nurturing one's well-being. Maria could prioritize her needs, pursue her passions, and create a unique and fulfilling life. She discovered happiness in the simplicity of these activities, relishing the freedom to explore new experiences without the limitations of a romantic partnership.

Embracing Freedom

Maria's journey was truly transformative, as she discovered the immense happiness accompanying freedom and self-reliance. She fully embraced the freedom to make choices driven by her desires and needs. Embarking on her inaugural solo journey, she ventured to the cities that had long captivated her imagination. She felt a rush of excitement and a newfound belief in herself. She discovered the art of exploring unfamiliar territories, connecting with unfamiliar faces, and relishing her solitude.

Maria's single status allowed her to prioritize her personal development. She immersed herself in literature, eagerly participating in workshops and delving into captivating subjects. She dedicated herself to her career, enrolling in courses that enhanced her skills and expanded her horizons. Through her dedication and hard work, she began to flourish both in her career and personal life.

Maria's tale beautifully captures the delightful and satisfying experiences that can arise when fully embracing a single life. Now is the perfect moment to prioritize self-discovery, pursue interests, and build a fulfilling and meaningful life. Maria's journey towards finding joy in her single life was not driven by a need to fill the void left by her marriage. Instead, it was a quest to uncover the richness and fulfillment of life on her terms.

Crafting a Meaningful Existence

Discovering the beauty of being single is a unique experience for each individual, often requiring a change in outlook. Viewing singleness as a valuable opportunity for growth and self-exploration, rather than a state of lack, can be a transformative perspective. It's an opportunity to reconnect with the things that bring you joy, to pursue interests that may have been put on hold, and to cultivate a strong sense of independence and fulfillment.

Maria's journey was genuinely life-changing. She discovered the beauty of solitude, embraced her artistic passions, and crafted a fulfilling existence brimming with delightful endeavors. She realized that her value did not depend on whether she was in a relationship. Instead, it was determined by the abundance of her life experiences and the strength of her self-acceptance.

The Power of Being Single

Discovering the happiness of being single is a truly empowering journey. It enables individuals to prioritize their needs and desires, leading a life aligned with their values and establishing confidence and self-worth. Now is the perfect moment to embrace your unique qualities, cultivate your interests, and savor the liberating feeling of being free.

Maria realized that being single is not a limitation but an opportunity to explore, grow, and thrive. It's a time in your life when you have the freedom to fully embrace your true self and build a life that is entirely your own. Embracing the path of self-discovery and savoring every moment of life is the key to finding happiness as a single individual, whether revisiting old hobbies or embarking on exciting new adventures.

Embarking on fresh hobbies and activities

Following the conclusion of a meaningful relationship, the idea of delving into fresh hobbies and activities can evoke a mix of anticipation and apprehension. During this time, people often embrace new experiences and rekindle their passion for personal interests. Exploring unknown territories can frequently result in surprising findings and personal development.

An Exciting Journey into the Unknown

Alex had always been an enthusiastic reader, but during his long-term relationship, he devoted most of his free time to activities his partner enjoyed. Following their separation, he realized that he had greatly overlooked his pursuits. With a strong desire to rediscover his identity, Alex chose to delve into various hobbies that had always piqued his curiosity yet had remained unexplored due to lack of time.

Photography became one of their newfound passions. Drawn to capture moments and perspectives, Alex purchased a pre-owned camera and began exploring his city through the lens. He started by capturing straightforward subjects - cityscapes, street scenes, and candid photographs of people. As he explored various methods and arrangements, he discovered a fresh avenue for showcasing his artistic flair. Photography became a source of solace, enabling him to view the world from a fresh perspective and find joy in the simple moments of life.

Exploring the Power of Community Through Fresh Interests

Alex's passion for photography also led him to join a local photography club. Initially, he felt a sense of apprehension about meeting unfamiliar faces, but he soon discovered that the group was hot and encouraging. He found solace in the club, where he could absorb knowledge from fellow members, showcase his creations, and receive valuable input. It also connected him with a group of like-minded people, providing some much-needed companionship after his relationship ended.

Alex took part in photo walks and exhibitions through the photography club. Engaging in these activities not only enhanced his abilities but also enhanced his social interactions. He discovered a circle of companions and immersed himself in thought-provoking discussions about art, creativity, and the complexities of existence. His horizons were expanded, and he found a renewed sense of purpose and connection.

Exploring New Horizons and Conquering Personal Challenges

Alex decided to step out of his comfort zone and take on a new challenge: rock climbing, in addition to his passion for photography. Despite his trepidation, he enrolled in a beginners' class at a nearby climbing gym. In the beginning, the initial sessions were quite daunting. However, thanks to the support and motivation from the instructors and fellow climbers, Alex conquered his fears gradually.

Alex gained valuable insights into resilience and perseverance through the experience of rock climbing. Every ascent symbolized triumph over challenges, whether on the rock face or in life's journey. With unwavering focus, immense strength, and an unyielding determination, he faced the physical challenge head-on. The nurturing and encouraging atmosphere of the climbing community provided him with the perfect platform to cultivate his self-assurance. Scaling new heights, Alex experienced a profound sense of achievement and empowerment that positively impacted various aspects of his life.

A Path of Rediscovery

Alex's exploration of different hobbies and activities went beyond acquiring new skills; it was a journey of self-discovery. By engaging in photography and rock climbing, he discovered the thrill of adventure and the bravery to venture beyond his familiar surroundings. These experiences reignited his curiosity and adventure, a powerful reminder that life is brimming with endless possibilities, even in the face of profound loss.

Exploring new hobbies allowed Alex to release the past and concentrate on the present. It enabled him to redirect his focus from what had been taken away to what could be acquired. Exploring new interests injected renewed enthusiasm into his life, enriching it with many uplifting moments and cherished memories.

Embracing Exciting Journeys

Discovering fresh interests and pastimes can be a transformative method for restoring self-worth and boosting confidence. It promotes personal development, nurtures imagination, and offers chances to connect with others and forge relationships. Alex found these new adventures to be life-changing. They supported him through his breakup, guided him in rediscovering his identity, and helped him develop a greater appreciation for life.

Embracing new hobbies requires an open mindset and willingness to try new things. Engaging in various activities, such as trying out a new sport, mastering a musical instrument, experimenting with different cuisines, or embarking on adventures to unfamiliar places, presents an opportunity for personal growth and self-discovery. Going through the ups and downs of life experiencing setbacks and triumphs, helps us develop inner strength and self-assurance. It shows us that there is still room for personal growth and happiness even after heartbreak.

The Joys of Discovery

Alex's story highlights the benefits of venturing into unfamiliar hobbies and activities. He stumbled upon hidden passions, forged fresh connections, and developed a stronger self-understanding. These fresh endeavors occupied his schedule and enhanced his existence, offering a profound meaning and satisfaction.

For those experiencing a similar journey, embracing the chance to explore fully is essential. After a breakup, life takes on a new chapter filled with opportunities for self-discovery and personal growth. By embracing new experiences and venturing into uncharted territory, many opportunities await you. Experience the chance to rekindle your passions, connect with individuals who share your interests, and, above all, embrace the sheer delight of living.

A Fresh Beginning

As Alex continued to delve into different interests, he realized that this phase of being alone was more than just a change but rather a fresh chapter in his journey. It was a time of embracing his unique identity, following his interests and living true to himself. His hobbies took on a deeper meaning as they reflected his personal growth, allowing him to cultivate a vibrant and fulfilling life that was truly his own.

Throughout this journey, Alex discovered that the conclusion of a relationship does not signify the conclusion of the tale. It's the start of an exciting journey, brimming with chances to learn, explore, and experience happiness. And in that thrilling journey, the possibilities are boundless.

Creating a Welcoming Community

Cultivating Strong Bonds with Friends and Loved Ones

Following a breakup, the presence of loved ones can provide immeasurable support as one navigates the path of healing and rediscovering self-worth. For countless individuals, their bonds with their loved ones are vital for strength and healing. Cultivating these relationships not only brings emotional solace but also aids in rekindling a sense of belonging and self-value.

The Familiarity of Long-time Companions

Lisa was always the center of attention, a social butterfly who loved being around people. Despite having many acquaintances, she felt isolated after her recent breakup. The once vibrant relationships now felt distant and superficial. Lisa realized that in her past relationships, she had slowly grown apart from her close friends, placing her partner above her long-standing friendships.

With a strong desire to rebuild connections, Lisa reached out to her dearest friends, who had consistently supported her throughout different stages of her life. She organized informal gatherings, ranging from meeting up for coffee to watching movies, where they could have open conversations and share laughter. These interactions were essential to Lisa, giving her a much-needed outlet to express herself, share her stories, and receive authentic support.

Sarah, one of her friends, noticed Lisa's need for emotional support and made it a point to check in regularly. Lisa found solace in their profound discussions and moments of shared joy, which aided her in navigating her feelings and reconstructing her identity. Sarah's compassionate nature and ability to truly understand others was a comforting reminder that, even though her relationship had ended, she still had a supportive network of people who genuinely cared about her.

Rekindling the ties that bind

The dynamics within her family greatly influenced Lisa's healing process. Throughout her relationship, she had grown somewhat distant from her family, placing more emphasis on her partner's family and their intertwined existence. Following the end of their relationship, she understood the significance of re-establishing a bond with her own family.

Lisa consciously prioritized quality time with her parents and siblings, taking the initiative to plan family dinners and arrange weekend visits. These moments brought her closer to her family and gave her the love and support she craved. Her parents, always a reliable source of guidance and support, provided words of motivation and practical suggestions. They served as a powerful reminder of her importance and the significance of maintaining strong bonds with those who have consistently supported her.

Building a Supportive Network

Aside from rekindling relationships with loved ones, Lisa was determined to forge new connections to foster her personal development. She became a member of a local book club and a yoga class, where she had the opportunity to connect with individuals who shared her passions. These newfound connections brought about new viewpoints and a feeling of belonging beyond her social circle.

Lisa's participation in these groups allowed her to form new connections and boosted her confidence. Being involved in these nurturing environments enabled her to participate in activities that brought her happiness and encouraged her personal growth. The connections she formed in these environments were rooted in shared passions and genuine admiration, which aided her in cultivating a supportive and uplifting community.

The Importance of Authentic Connections

Lisa's story emphasizes the significance of fostering authentic relationships. Authentic friendships and nurturing family connections go beyond mere social interactions; they are vital in maintaining emotional well-being. They offer a secure environment where you can freely express your true self, discuss your challenges, and receive uplifting support.

Lisa discovered solace and strength by prioritizing the quality of her relationships over quantity. She found the true worth of a handful of meaningful connections, realizing they hold more value than many superficial ones. Those who supported her during the breakup were a powerful reminder of her value and the profound influence of authentic connections on her journey to healing.

The Strength of Collective Assistance

Building a supportive community relies heavily on mutual support, which plays a crucial role in recovery. Lisa's friends and family played a significant role in supporting her throughout her healing journey. They rejoiced in her accomplishments, offered support during difficult times, and fostered a feeling of inclusion. Lisa's confidence was restored, and she felt a sense of worth through the support she received, which highlighted the significance of fostering meaningful connections.

Embracing the Power of Togetherness

Lisa's story highlights the importance of embracing and fostering a supportive community. The connections she reignited and the fresh ones she forged were vital in her quest to reconstruct self-worth and assurance. Surrounded by a caring and supportive circle, she discovered the strength to push ahead and reconnect with her true identity.

Creating and fostering a supportive community is a continuous endeavor. It requires looking for assistance and being willing to provide it in return. Lisa's story beautifully showcases the power of fostering connections, which can lead to a harmonious cycle of encouragement, benefiting both oneself and those around us, enabling personal growth and emotional healing.

An Endless Adventure

Creating a nurturing community is a lifelong endeavor. Dedication, a receptive attitude, and a readiness to prioritize meaningful connections. Lisa found that reconnecting with friends and family and forming new connections played a crucial role in her healing journey. She was able to rekindle the delight of authentic friendship and experience the power of being part of a supportive community.

In the end, fostering friendships and family relationships is about discovering a feeling of belonging and support that enhances your life. It's all about building a community of individuals who support and motivate you, guiding you toward regaining self-esteem and love after experiencing a difficult time. As Lisa's story illustrates, these connections prove to be priceless in healing and personal development, offering a solid base of resilience and motivation for what lies ahead.

Looking for Professional Assistance (Therapy, Coaching)

After experiencing a significant breakup, many people find it helpful to seek professional support as they work towards rebuilding their self-love and confidence. Therapy and coaching provide essential guidance and tools for navigating the intricacies of emotional recovery, which many find invaluable. This aspect of the journey has the power to bring about profound change, offering a well-defined route towards healing and individual development.

A Turning Point: Seeking Help

Rachel was overcome with a profound sense of sadness and confusion following the end of her long-term relationship. Despite the unwavering support from loved ones, she found it challenging to overcome the pain of her shattered heart. She was burdened by the weight of unresolved issues and lingering doubts about herself, which started to feel overwhelming. One day, a dear friend recommended that Rachel talk to a therapist.

Rachel was initially unsure. She was concerned about the negative connotations surrounding therapy and had doubts about its effectiveness. After careful consideration and recognizing that she required additional assistance beyond her close network, she sought professional support.

Discovering the Perfect Match

Rachel embarked on her quest for a therapist by conducting thorough research online and seeking valuable recommendations.

She carefully considered finding someone whose approach aligned with her values and who had expertise in addressing relationship challenges and building self-confidence. After careful consideration, she selected a therapist who specialized in cognitive-behavioral therapy (CBT) and was compassionate and understanding.

Rachel experienced a blend of nervousness and comfort during the initial sessions. The therapist created a secure environment for Rachel to delve into her emotions, recognize harmful thought patterns, and navigate through the burdensome feelings she had been experiencing. Through each session, Rachel delved into profound realizations about her actions and convictions, leading her to grasp the underlying causes of her heartbreak and self-doubt.

Exploring the Therapeutic Journey

Rachel found therapy to be a helpful way to tackle her problems systematically. The therapist employed a range of techniques to assist her in questioning negative thoughts and cultivating more effective ways of dealing with challenges. Rachel found journaling a transformative exercise, enabling her to express her emotions and contemplate her growth.

Rachel gained essential skills in handling anxiety and developing self-confidence. Her therapist introduced mindfulness practices and self-compassion exercises, which became crucial for navigating her emotional landscape. During this journey, Rachel began to see herself in a more compassionate and empathetic light, slowly constructing a more optimistic perception of herself.

The Importance of Coaching

Alongside therapy, Rachel explored life coaching as an additional form of support. She found a coach who had expertise in personal development and setting goals. Unlike therapy, which primarily dealt with past issues and emotional healing, coaching offered Rachel practical strategies to set and achieve new goals.

Rachel's life coach assisted her in developing a plan to foster her personal development. They focused on establishing immediate and future objectives, creating strategies for implementation, and promoting a mentality of strength and self-empowerment. Rachel found the coaching sessions to be invigorating and future-oriented, inspiring her to imagine a life beyond her previous relationship.

Combining Therapy and Coaching for a Holistic Approach

Rachel found that the combination of therapy and coaching was beneficial. Through treatment, she was able to heal from past wounds and gain a deeper understanding of herself. However, coaching was crucial in providing her the motivation and direction to pursue new aspirations. These approaches worked together to establish a support system that thoroughly covered emotional healing and practical growth.

Creating a Support Network

Rachel's experience with professional support highlighted the significance of incorporating therapy and coaching into her current support network. She continued cultivating her friendships and family relationships, sharing her journey with those who held her dear. With the help of expert advice and close relationships, she found a strong support network that played a crucial role in her journey towards recovery.

The Significance of Professional Assistance

Rachel's story showcases the profound influence that therapy and coaching can have on restoring self-love and confidence. Professional assistance provided her a secure environment to delve into her emotions, acquire understanding, and create effective progress methods. It gave her the strength to face her past, embrace her abilities, and envision her future.

Embracing the Adventure

Reaching out for professional support shows excellent strength and a proactive approach towards healing. It represents a dedication to personal development and a readiness to invest in oneself. For individuals going through the aftermath of a breakup, therapy and coaching offer valuable tools and resources to help overcome challenges and rebuild a sense of self-worth.

Rachel's story exemplifies professional support's profound impact on one's life. Through the power of therapy and coaching, she found the strength to overcome her past, regain her self-assurance, and embrace a future filled with personal development and endless opportunities.

An Enduring Asset

Therapy and coaching offer long-term support for personal growth and overall well-being, extending beyond temporary fixes. Rachel benefits from the skills and insights acquired through these processes, which help her tackle new challenges and seize opportunities. Her story highlights the importance of reaching out to professionals and incorporating their guidance into one's journey of self-discovery and empowerment.

Pursuing therapy and coaching can be a transformative move toward regaining self-love and confidence. It unlocks the door to a life-changing journey of healing, personal development, and rejuvenation, leading to a brighter and more satisfying future.

PART 3
Preparing For New Love

PREPARING NEW LOVE

Prepare your heart for new love by defining what you truly desire, setting healthy boundaries, and embracing vulnerability—laying the foundation for a deeper, more fulfilling connection in your next relationship

Defining Your Ideal Relationship

Getting to Know Your Needs and Desires

As you begin your quest for new love, fully comprehend your needs and desires. Embarking on this journey of self-discovery sets the stage for a meaningful connection that brings joy to your heart and resonates with your individual development and principles. It's about imagining a collaboration that enriches your life instead of making it more complex.

Self-Discovery Unveiled

Having gone through a period of healing and personal growth, Emily was now prepared to embrace the potential of new opportunities. After a profound personal transformation, she realized the importance of clarifying her relationship desires before re-entering the dating scene. Emily had gained valuable insights from her previous relationships, and she was excited to put this newfound wisdom into practice.

She started by dedicating a portion of her weekly schedule to contemplating her experiences and aspirations. Amidst these quiet moments, Emily would reflect on her thoughts, pondering significant questions: What qualities held the utmost importance in a potential companion? What were the things she refused to compromise on? What factors contribute to her sense of fulfillment in a relationship?

Delving into the Essence of Values

Emily realized that grasping her core values was crucial to establishing her perfect relationship. She listed a few important values that she hoped to find in her future partner: respect, honesty, and the opportunity for personal development. Looking back on her past relationships, she couldn't help but notice how the differences in values had significantly affected her overall dissatisfaction. With this newfound clarity, she could direct her attention to the things that mattered.

She delved into the significance of emotional compatibility. Emily desired a companion who possessed both kindness and supportiveness and a shared enthusiasm for personal development and growth. She imagined a connection where both individuals could motivate one another to reach their aspirations and face life's obstacles as a team.

Identify Your Relationship Objectives

She embarked on a journey to comprehend better her needs and desires, which also entailed recognizing her relationship goals. She desired a collaboration to encourage her ambitions while nurturing a deep sense of unity. She considered factors like long-term compatibility, life plans, and how they matched up with her partner's vision.

One evening, Emily found herself peaceful, sipping a warm cup of tea and reflecting in her journal. In that serene atmosphere, she decided to map out her relationship aspirations. She longed for a relationship built on shared interests and mutual admiration. She imagined a future where she and her partner could create a life together, merging their dreams and encouraging each other's aspirations.

The Importance of Personal Development

Her personal growth greatly influenced Emily's understanding of her ideal relationship. Through therapy, coaching, and self-reflection, she gained valuable experiences and insights to determine her true desires confidently. She understood that a positive relationship would support her personal development instead of holding her back.

Emily recognized the significance of emotional intelligence and effective communication in a relationship. She desired a companion who could participate in candid and sincere discussions, handle disagreements positively, and provide mutual emotional support. These elements became essential to her conception of a satisfying relationship.

Imagining the Perfect Match

Emily created a list of qualities and attributes she wanted in a partner to understand her vision better. She pictured someone who was supportive and caring, had a great sense of humor, shared her values, and had similar interests. Through this exercise, she was able to form a vivid image of the ideal individual who would perfectly complement her life and bring even more joy into it.

Emily's journey of self-discovery involved discovering what she truly wanted and needed in a relationship rather than seeking perfection. She focused on identifying the qualities that foster a positive and fulfilling partnership. She had to truly understand herself to find a partner who shared her values and aspirations.

Vision Alignment

Emily's newfound clarity about her needs and desires instilled confidence and readiness within her to embark on a journey to find a new relationship. She understood that determining her perfect relationship was an ongoing journey, necessitating constant self-awareness and flexibility. Emily's unwavering commitment to her values and aspirations paved the way for a partnership that would fulfill her requirements and bring immense fulfillment to her life.

Unleashing the Power of Self-Knowledge

Emily's story showcases the importance of understanding oneself when ready for a new romantic relationship. Through a deep understanding of her needs and desires, she approached the dating world with a clear sense of purpose. Her newfound self-awareness gave her the confidence to pursue relationships that matched her vision and added to her happiness.

Emily eagerly anticipated the arrival of new love, embracing the journey with a positive and open mindset. She understood that comprehending her needs and desires was crucial to building a satisfying relationship. Emily's unwavering commitment to her values, aspirations, and self-improvement paved the way for a fulfilling partnership to enrich her life and fill it with happiness.

Determining your ideal relationship goes beyond imagining a flawless partner; it involves gaining insight into yourself and recognizing what you require to flourish in a relationship. Emily's story is a powerful reminder of the importance of self-discovery when finding love. It shows us that we can create a foundation for a meaningful and rewarding partnership by genuinely knowing ourselves.

Establishing Healthy Boundaries

As you embark on a journey of new love, establishing healthy boundaries becomes a vital part of shaping your perfect relationship. Boundaries are not about constructing barriers; instead, they involve establishing a space where both partners can feel a sense of respect, appreciation, and the freedom to express their true selves. Understanding and establishing boundaries can be a transformative step towards nurturing a healthy and fulfilling relationship, especially for those who have experienced past heartbreak.

Discovering the Importance of Personal Boundaries

Following her recent breakup, Lisa was relentless in her determination to approach her subsequent relationship with a fresh perspective and a clear understanding of herself. Through her previous relationship, she gained valuable insights into the significance of establishing and upholding healthy boundaries. As Lisa reflected on her experiences, she realized she frequently faced challenges when expressing her needs and setting boundaries. This occasionally resulted in feelings of frustration and a lack of equilibrium.

Lisa embarked on her journey, delving into the idea of limits and borders. She grasped the importance of boundaries, recognizing that they were not meant to be strict or domineering but to facilitate open and effective communication of each partner's desires and expectations. Her goal was to create a solid foundation where respect and understanding were the main pillars of the relationship.

Exploring the Boundaries of Personal Capacity

To establish healthy boundaries, Lisa had to understand her limitations and requirements clearly. She dedicated a moment to ponder over the difficulties she had encountered in her past relationships and contemplated the changes she desired for the future. Through this introspection, she discovered a few crucial aspects that required her to set firmer limits.

For example, Lisa realized that she frequently overlooked her time and space in her past relationship, placing her partner's needs above hers. She realized that finding a harmonious equilibrium between her personal and shared time was paramount for her well-being and happiness. Recognizing this, Lisa established limits that would enable her to preserve her individuality and freedom.

Effective Communication of Boundaries

After better grasping her needs, Lisa shifted her focus towards effectively expressing her boundaries in future relationships. She understood the importance of openly and honestly communicating boundaries to foster a strong and healthy partnership. She worked on expressing her needs in a considerate and confident manner, with the goal of creating a safe space for open communication about their mutual expectations.

Lisa recognized the importance of having adaptable and open boundaries. She understood the importance of compromise in relationships and the need for open communication to navigate differing perspectives and needs. She aimed to establish a safe environment where she and her partner could freely communicate their boundaries without any concerns of criticism or disagreement.

Illustrations of Strong Boundaries

Lisa began to detail particular limits she wished to set in her future relationship. As an illustration, she prioritized regular "me time" to dedicate herself to her hobbies and interests, recognizing the importance of maintaining her mental and emotional well-being. She also made it a point to ensure that her partner understood and respected her personal space and privacy boundaries.

In addition, Lisa expressed a desire to establish clear guidelines for communication. She appreciated the importance of open and honest conversations and recognized the need to set boundaries for discussing sensitive topics. Lisa sought to establish clear communication boundaries to foster a harmonious and considerate conversation that catered to the emotional needs of both partners.

Exploring the Importance of Boundaries in Establishing Trust

Lisa's story underscored the importance of establishing clear boundaries to foster trust in a relationship. Setting clear boundaries was essential for creating a secure and respectful environment and nurturing a deep emotional bond. Lisa's precise definition of her needs and limits fostered an environment of trust and security, ensuring that both partners felt valued.

Overcoming Obstacles and Making Adaptations

As Lisa began her adventure into a new romance, she realized that establishing and upholding boundaries would necessitate continuous dedication and open dialogue. She was ready to tackle obstacles and adapt as necessary, understanding that limits were not fixed but changed over time as the connection developed.

Lisa understood the significance of mutual respect in maintaining healthy boundaries. She was dedicated to understanding her partner's needs and boundaries and finding a harmonious balance with her own. The collaborative approach played a crucial role in establishing a nurturing and sustainable relationship.

Embracing the Journey with a Sense of Assurance

With a fresh perspective on personal limits, Lisa began her quest for love with a sense of assurance and a clear vision. She embraced entering relationships with a strong sense of self and dedication to prioritizing her well-being. Lisa established clear boundaries, which formed the foundation for a relationship that respected her values and encouraged her personal development.

The Power of Setting Boundaries

Lisa's story highlights the profound impact of establishing healthy boundaries in shaping your desired relationship. Boundaries are not meant to restrict but to establish a nurturing environment where both partners can flourish. They foster open, sincere communication, mutual admiration, and a stronger emotional bond.

Embracing Vulnerability

The Importance of Vulnerability in Building Meaningful Connections

As you embark on a new chapter of love, embracing vulnerability becomes crucial in forging profound and meaningful connections. Sharing your true self with someone else requires a willingness to be open and exposed, even when you feel delicate. Through this willingness to be vulnerable, genuine closeness and connection can flourish, resulting in a profoundly satisfying and life-changing relationship.

Following her breakup, Emma approached her future relationship sincerely and transparently. Through her previous encounters, she understood that embracing vulnerability could present difficulties and offer great fulfillment. Emma had frequently suppressed her genuine emotions and thoughts, plagued by the fear of being judged or rejected. Yet, she realized that opening herself to vulnerability was crucial in establishing a more profound bond with a potential companion.

Emma embarked on her journey, taking a moment to ponder the significance of vulnerability in her life. She grasped the importance of embracing vulnerability, which demanded bravery and a deep understanding of oneself. Sharing her fears, dreams, and insecurities with someone she deeply cared for and embracing her true self was integral to her journey.

The Advantages of Embracing Openness

Emma discovered the power of vulnerability in fostering deep connections with others through her personal journey. She understood that being open and honest creates an environment of trust and closeness, enabling both individuals to form a stronger bond. Emma's willingness to be vulnerable also allowed her partner to open up, fostering an environment where they both felt safe to be their genuine selves.

As Emma settled down for the evening, journal in hand and a warm cup of tea, she lost herself in contemplation. Her thoughts wandered to the precious moments in her past relationships, where the power of vulnerability had forged more profound connections with her partners. She recalled the moments when they had opened up to each other, forging a deep connection built on mutual understanding and empathy. These experiences solidified her conviction in the strength of being open and exposed.

Conquering the Dread of Being Turned Down

Emma struggled with her fear of rejection, even though she had developed a deeper understanding of vulnerability. She understood the potential consequences of vulnerability, aware that it could lead to pain or misinterpretation. Her past experiences had frequently hindered her, leading her to construct barriers to protect herself emotionally.

To conquer this fear, Emma dedicated herself to practicing self-compassion and consistently reminded herself that vulnerability should not be seen as a weakness but as a source of strength. She understood that not every connection would result in the desired outcome, but she believed being open and authentic was crucial to finding a meaningful relationship. Emma embraced a new mindset, recognizing vulnerability as a brave form of self-expression rather than something to fear.

Establishing a Safe Environment

Emma recognized the significance of establishing a safe and trusting atmosphere as she prepared to open herself up to vulnerability in her future relationship. She understood the importance of creating an environment where both partners felt respected and valued, as vulnerability flourished in such a space. Emma was determined to cultivate a climate of honest dialogue and shared comprehension in her forthcoming relationship.

Emma pondered the delicate art of maintaining vulnerability while also establishing healthy boundaries. She understood the importance of balancing openness with self-respect and autonomy. She intended to convey her emotions and personal encounters in a manner that was genuine and respectful of her partner's feelings and limits.

A Delicate Dance

Emma's journey shed light on the ever-changing nature of vulnerability within relationships. It's a beautiful dance of reciprocity, where partners gracefully alternate between being open and supportive. Emma grasped the importance of mutual effort and reciprocity regarding vulnerability. The focus was on establishing an environment where both partners felt comfortable expressing their thoughts and emotions without any concerns about being judged or criticized.

Emma daydreamed about the type of connection she longed for, which valued openness and vulnerability as essential elements of closeness. She imagined a collaboration where she and her partner could freely discuss their dreams, fears, and aspirations, deepening their bond through mutual understanding and empathy.

Embracing vulnerability as a pathway to personal growth

Emma eagerly embraced vulnerability as she prepared to embark on a new chapter in her love life, recognizing it as a powerful catalyst for personal and relational growth. She understood that being genuine and vulnerable would strengthen her bond with a potential partner and improve her emotional state. Emma's decision to reveal her true self catalyzed a genuinely authentic and satisfying connection.

The Power of Vulnerability: A Life-Changing Journey

Emma's story highlights vulnerability's profound impact on forging meaningful relationships. We open the door to genuine connections and deep understanding by embracing vulnerability. Opening ourselves up to vulnerability creates a deep connection with others, leading to significant and long-lasting relationships.

As you embark on a new romantic journey, embracing vulnerability can pave the way for a deeper and more fulfilling connection. When you embrace vulnerability and show your true self, you create an opportunity for a meaningful and satisfying connection. This kind of relationship allows you and your partner to flourish and evolve together.

Conquering the Apprehension of Experiencing Pain Once More

Embarking on a fresh romance following a painful breakup often entails facing the apprehension of getting hurt once more. Fear can frequently act as a formidable obstacle, preventing us from fully embracing vulnerability and experiencing authentic connections. Nevertheless, confronting and conquering this fear is essential for embracing new opportunities and fostering a relationship founded on trust and vulnerability.

The Burden of Previous Injuries

Following a painful betrayal in her previous relationship, Sarah approached the idea of opening her heart again with caution. Her past haunted her, leaving a lasting impact on her thoughts and actions. She discovered herself always on edge, fearful that any fresh connection could result in comparable anguish.

The intensity of Sarah's fear was undeniable. Whenever she thought about starting a new relationship, she would relive painful memories of heartbreak, experiencing the same feelings of betrayal as if they were occurring in the present moment. Her fear hindered her ability to fully immerse herself in the present and welcome the possibility of new love.

A Tale of Healing

Sarah realized that to conquer her fear of being hurt once more, she had to set out on a healing path. She started by recognizing her emotions and permitting herself to mourn the end of her previous relationship. Embracing this process of acceptance proved crucial in propelling us forward. With the help of therapy and introspection, Sarah dedicated herself to unraveling the depths of her fears and how they influenced her capacity to form meaningful connections with those around her.

As Sarah jotted down her thoughts in her journal, she suddenly realized. It dawned on her that her fear extended beyond mere physical pain; it also encompassed the idea of being vulnerable. She observed the consequences of her apprehension, realizing that it had caused her to construct emotional barriers. These walls shielded her from potential pain but also prevented her from forging deep and meaningful relationships.

Developing Strong Emotional Resilience

Sarah made it a priority to develop emotional resilience to confront her fear. She consciously cared for herself and participated in activities that boosted her belief in herself and her abilities. Sarah started establishing achievable objectives to slowly embrace unfamiliar situations and connections, allowing herself to explore vulnerability securely and measuredly.

Sarah's journey involved discovering the fine line between being cautious and being overwhelmed by fear. She realized being cautious was a natural response, but she understood that letting fear control her actions would only hinder her progress. Sarah's journey towards emotional resilience and regained confidence began with her willingness to embrace vulnerability through small steps.

The Importance of Trust

Sarah understood the importance of rebuilding trust to conquer her fear. She began her journey by building self-confidence and her ability to make sound decisions. Sarah was determined to trust her instincts and establish limits safeguarding her emotional health. She discovered the importance of relying on her instincts to navigate relationships while respecting her boundaries and limitations.

Sarah approached her interactions with potential partners with a focus on gradually establishing trust. She understood the importance of building trust over time and letting relationships develop organically. Sarah established a solid base for trust to flourish by prioritizing open and respectful communication.

Confronting Fear as a Team

As Sarah embarked on her journey into the dating world, she embraced new relationships with optimism and a willingness to be vulnerable. She communicated openly about her past experiences and fears, ensuring that both parties agreed. She discovered the importance of opening up to her partner, creating a space where they could openly discuss their worries and support each other through their vulnerabilities. Sarah found solace in this approach, as she received the support and understanding she needed instead of confronting her fears alone.

During an early conversation with a new partner, Sarah openly discussed her previous heartbreak and her fears. Her partner's response was a source of relief for her. They showed understanding and comfort, recognizing her emotions and affirming their dedication to fostering a relationship grounded in trust and mutual assistance. This experience strengthened Sarah's conviction that embracing vulnerability can result in positive outcomes and encourage more profound connections.

Embracing the Potential for Happiness

Sarah's path to conquering her fear of getting hurt once more brought her to a powerful revelation: although pain was a potential outcome, so was the experience of joy. She realized that embracing vulnerability also exposed her to the potential for a rewarding and affectionate connection. Sarah shifted her perspective and prioritized the possibilities of happiness and personal development rather than getting caught up in the negative emotions of past pain.

As Sarah continued her journey, she discovered that embracing vulnerability led to meaningful connections. She realized confronting her fears with bravery opened doors to deeper connections and insights. Through facing her fears and embracing the potential for happiness, Sarah opened herself up to a relationship that brought immense fulfillment and personal growth.

Embracing the Potential of Confronting Fear

Sarah's story showcases the incredible impact of confronting the fear of getting hurt once more. By facing our fears and embracing vulnerability, we can experience deep and satisfying connections with others. Through developing emotional resilience, cultivating trust, and embracing the potential for joy, we have the power to conquer the obstacles that hinder us and establish an environment where new love can thrive.

As you embark on the path of new love, it's important to remember that conquering the apprehension of getting hurt once more is a process that demands patience and bravery. Embracing vulnerability, confronting your fears, and opening yourself up to the richness of connection will result in an incredibly fulfilling and profoundly life-changing relationship.

The Significance of Effective Communication

Developing Strong Communication Abilities

Effective communication is crucial for building a solid foundation in any successful relationship. As you embark on a new romantic journey, it is vital to refine your communication skills. Developing the skill to communicate effectively, actively listen, and engage in conversations with empathy can lead to a stronger and more meaningful bond with a potential partner.

An Exploration of Communication Needs

Following the unfortunate end of her previous relationship, Rachel approached her next romantic endeavor with a renewed understanding of the significance of effective communication. She realized that a lack of open communication about their needs, expectations, and feelings was the root cause of many problems. Rachel had a moment of realization that changed everything. She understood the importance of effective communication in maintaining a solid and enduring relationship.

Rachel embarked on a journey driven by her determination to enhance her communication skills. She began by looking back at her previous discussions and pinpointing the areas where she faced difficulties. Rachel realized that she frequently struggled to convey her emotions and needs, resulting in misunderstandings and unresolved conflicts.

The Importance of Active Listening

Rachel embarked on her journey to develop practical communication skills by mastering the art of active listening. She realized that the art of listening extended beyond mere auditory perception, encompassing a deep comprehension of the speaker's point of view. Rachel honed her listening ability, refraining from interrupting and giving her partner the space to fully express themselves before responding. She was utterly absorbed in the present moment, fully engaged in the conversation.

During a casual conversation with a dear friend, Rachel used active listening techniques. She discovered that she could participate in a more profound and significant discussion by entirely focusing on her friend and carefully considering what was shared. This experience highlighted the importance of attentive listening and how it builds authentic relationships.

Communicating Your Thoughts and Feelings with Clarity and Sincerity

Rachel tried to improve her communication skills, ensuring she expressed herself clearly and honestly. She grasped the importance of effective communication, realizing that expressing her thoughts and emotions in an assertive yet respectful manner was crucial. Rachel embarked on a journey to master the art of expressing her needs and setting boundaries, free from any apprehension of being judged or encountering conflict.

Rachel emphasized the use of "I" statements in her conversations, specifically expressing her emotions and desires by saying things like "I feel" or "I need." By adopting this approach, she effectively conveyed her point of view without coming across as accusatory or aggressive. Rachel discovered that this approach encouraged a greater level of open and productive conversation, enabling her to tackle problems with clarity and comprehension effectively.

Handling Challenging Discussions

Rachel understood the importance of skillfully handling challenging discussions with tact and understanding. She understood that conflicts and disagreements were bound to happen in any relationship and that positively dealing with them was crucial for maintaining a solid connection.

Rachel diligently honed her ability to remain calm and composed in anticipation of difficult discussions. She approached conflicts with a problem-solving mindset, prioritizing finding solutions over assigning blame. Rachel discovered the importance of acknowledging and respecting her partner's emotions and viewpoints, even if they didn't align with hers. Her compassionate approach enabled her to tackle issues in a manner that cultivated a sense of mutual respect and comprehension.

Fostering a Culture of Open Communication

Rachel recognized the importance of fostering an atmosphere that promotes open dialogue to develop practical communication skills. Her goal was to foster a connection where both individuals could freely share their thoughts, emotions, and worries without fearing criticism or retaliation.

Rachel realized that unexpressed expectations and assumptions often impeded effective communication in her previous relationship. She was dedicated to creating a space where she and her partner could freely communicate their wants and needs. Rachel imagined a collaboration where frequent updates and honest discussions were woven into the very essence of the relationship, guaranteeing that both partners stayed on the same page and connected.

Embracing the Journey of Constant Improvement

Rachel understood that effective communication was a skill that needed constant development and refinement. She embarked on her journey with an open mind, ready to absorb new knowledge and adjust as needed. She recognized that effective communication required continuous dedication and a deep understanding of oneself. Rachel committed to actively seeking feedback from her partner and remained open to adjusting her communication style as necessary.

Rachel actively sought opportunities for personal growth, including attending workshops and immersing herself in books on communication. The resources offered valuable insights and tools that enhanced her understanding of effective communication and its importance in fostering strong relationships.

The Power of Communication to Create Change

Rachel's experience highlights the profound impact that can be achieved by developing strong communication abilities. Through prioritizing active listening, effective communication, and empathetic navigation of challenging discussions, she readied herself for a relationship that could foster authentic connection and shared understanding.

As you embark on a new journey of love, it's essential to remember that effective communication goes beyond mere words. It involves building a stronger bond by truly understanding and empathizing with each other. Developing practical communication skills establishes a solid basis for a satisfying and long-lasting relationship. This allows for a partnership in which you and your partner can flourish and prosper together.

Handling Challenging Dialogues

Handling challenging discussions is crucial to getting ready for a new relationship. It's more than just talking about light-hearted subjects; it's about approaching intricate and occasionally uncomfortable matters with compassion and comprehension. Developing proficiency in this skill can turn potential conflicts into chances for stronger bonds and shared development.

Confronting the Obvious Issue

Following the end of her previous relationship, which was marred by unresolved conflicts, Laura became acutely conscious of the significance of confronting difficult conversations directly in her future relationship. She recalled the countless instances when she had steered clear of addressing delicate subjects, holding onto the belief that staying quiet would somehow resolve the problems. On the contrary, these discussions frequently escalated and became increasingly intricate, resulting in more harm than benefit.

With a firm resolve, Laura chose to face this challenge head-on. She started by recognizing that avoiding challenging discussions would only result in further complications. With this understanding, Laura braced herself for the unavoidable obstacles accompanying discussing challenging topics in a relationship.

The Mastery of Serenity

Laura's initial approach to handling challenging discussions involved mastering the skill of maintaining composure. She understood the importance of staying calm to have a meaningful conversation. During heightened emotions, discussions frequently descended into heated debates or miscommunications. To address this, Laura consciously incorporated deep breathing and mindfulness techniques into her routine, allowing her to maintain control over her emotions.

One evening, as she got ready to discuss her hopes for future commitments with a potential partner, Laura reminded herself to remain level-headed. Before the conversation, she paused to take a few deep breaths, ensuring she was calm and focused. Her thorough preparation allowed her to express her thoughts composed and effectively, establishing a favorable atmosphere for the conversation.

Engaging with Compassion

Listening with empathy is a crucial aspect of successfully navigating challenging conversations. Laura discovered the significance of comprehending her partner's point of view, realizing that it was equally essential to expressing her emotions. By actively listening, she could fully understand the other person's worries and feelings, which helped to create a strong sense of respect between them.

During one of her initial discussions with a new partner, Laura deliberately chose to actively listen without interrupting. She consciously tried to comprehend their perspective and acknowledge their emotions, even if they didn't align with hers. The issue was successfully resolved by taking an empathetic approach, and the connection between both partners was strengthened. It was clear that both perspectives were highly valued.

Resolving Problems in a Productive Manner

Laura understood the significance of approaching problems constructively. Instead of pointing fingers or making accusations, she focused on shaping the conversation around discovering solutions and empathizing with each other's needs. She expressed her feelings and concerns using "I" statements in a non-confrontational manner.

When talking about a disagreement regarding personal boundaries, Laura expressed her discomfort with sudden changes in plans. She emphasized the need for more time to adjust, effectively communicating her needs without criticizing her partner. This approach fostered a productive and respectful dialogue.

The Importance of Timing

The timing of specific conversations proved essential in successfully navigating challenging situations. Laura discovered the importance of timing when it comes to discussing sensitive topics in order to have a fruitful discussion. Opting for a moment when both partners were relaxed and not preoccupied with other sources of stress contributed to establishing a more favorable setting for a meaningful conversation.

On a specific evening, Laura and her partner had scheduled a conversation about their future aspirations. Sensing their calm and upbeat demeanor, Laura decided it was the perfect time to discuss the topic. At this particular moment, they found themselves in a position where they could have a sincere and genuine discussion, free from the burdens of immediate tension or interruptions.

Discovering Shared Perspectives

As Laura embarked on her quest to navigate challenging discussions, she made it a priority to seek out areas of agreement. She engaged in conversations to foster mutual understanding and consensus. Laura and her partner collaborated effectively by finding common ground and working towards their shared objectives.

While discussing their relationship, Laura emphasized their shared goal of having a supportive and committed partnership. Through their shared goal, they reached a compromise that satisfied both parties, strengthening their connection and showcasing the effectiveness of working together to solve problems.

The Impact of Open Dialogue on Personal Growth

Laura's experience highlights the profound impact of open and honest dialogue when navigating challenging discussions. Laura successfully navigated difficult conversations with self-assurance and poise by maintaining composure, showing understanding, positively handling problems, and selecting opportune moments.

As you embark on a new chapter of love, it's essential to remember that handling challenging discussions isn't about evading conflict but embracing the chance for personal development and deeper connection. By mastering this skill, a solid foundation is established for a relationship in which both partners can effectively navigate challenges with empathy and mutual respect, resulting in a more profound and satisfying connection.

PART 4
Navigating New Relationships

Starting Fresh: The First Steps

Tips for Dating After Heartbreak

Starting afresh after a painful breakup can evoke a mix of emotions - a blend of anticipation and trepidation. Embarking on a journey of connecting with someone new can evoke excitement and nervousness. It's a path that demands a delicate blend of bravery, introspection, and perseverance. Discover valuable insights and tips for navigating the dating world following a painful breakup.

Getting back into the dating scene

Following the end of a significant relationship, Daniel discovered a sense of caution when re-entering the dating scene. Haunted by the memories of his past relationship, he found himself treading carefully when forming new connections. Nevertheless, he understood that isolating himself was not the solution. He approached the dating scene cautiously, taking care not to overwhelm himself.

Daniel started by establishing modest, attainable objectives. Instead of immediately jumping into a serious dating scene, he decided to ease into it by participating in more relaxed social activities. For instance, he joined a hiking group and attended casual get-togethers with friends. These events created a calm atmosphere for him to hone his social skills and make new acquaintances. It was a turning point for Daniel, restoring his self-assurance and showing him that dating could be a delightful and carefree experience.

A Moment of Contemplation

One of the critical steps Daniel took was allowing himself to contemplate his true desires in a relationship. Reflecting on past relationships is crucial after experiencing heartbreak. It's essential to analyze what aspects were successful and what aspects were not. Daniel dedicated time to reflecting on his past experiences, recognizing recurring themes, and contemplating his top priorities as a potential partner.

It dawned on him that he frequently sacrificed his needs to satisfy his partner in his past relationship. Through this reflection, he better understood his personal boundaries and the specific qualities he desired in a potential new relationship. Through gaining a clear understanding of his own desires and deal-breakers, Daniel felt more self-assured and purposeful when making decisions about his dating life.

Sharing the Truth and Being Transparent

As Daniel started getting to know new people, he deliberately chose to be sincere and transparent about his past experiences and intentions. He recognized the value of honesty in establishing a passionate bond. Daniel was open about his past experiences of being hurt, but he preferred not to focus on them.

During his initial dates, Daniel mentioned that he had recently ended a long-term relationship and preferred to proceed cautiously. He discovered that being truthful created a favorable atmosphere and encouraged more genuine discussions. It also allowed him to assess how potential partners responded to his honesty, giving him a glimpse into their communication preferences and levels of compassion.

Embracing the Journey of Learning

Dating after experiencing heartbreak can be a valuable learning experience. Daniel soon realized that not every date would result in a profound bond, which was perfectly acceptable. He embraced every new encounter with a sense of wonder and a willingness to explore, viewing it as a chance to gain deeper insights into himself and his desires within a relationship.

Daniel learned a valuable lesson about communication from a memorable date. He went out with someone who, although they had a charming and exciting personality, frequently interrupted him during conversations. Although the date didn't result in a follow-up encounter, it only strengthened Daniel's longing for a companion who truly appreciated the importance of attentive listening and considerate communication. Every experience, whether a success or a setback, contributed to Daniel's growth and deepened his understanding of his desires.

Enjoying a Leisurely Pace

One of the critical lessons Daniel learned was the value of being patient and taking things at a slower pace. Following a painful experience, seeking solace and security in a fresh connection is only natural. On the other hand, acting hastily may result in repeating familiar patterns or disregarding crucial warning signs. Daniel chose to be deliberate in getting to know potential partners.

He embraced the joy of dating, prioritizing the journey over the destination. Daniel established personal guidelines, such as restricting the frequency of his dates and allowing himself sufficient time to reflect on each encounter. By adopting this approach, he could establish meaningful connections at a natural and genuine pace without the need to rush into anything too serious.

Remaining Authentic to Your Identity

One of the critical lessons that Daniel learned was the significance of remaining authentic to who he truly is. In previous experiences, he occasionally found himself losing touch with his sense of self within relationships, exerting excessive effort to conform to the expectations of others. On this occasion, Daniel relentlessly committed to staying genuine and authentic to his principles.

He took the time to look after himself and prioritized his well-being. Daniel remained dedicated to his hobbies and interests, ensuring a harmonious equilibrium between his romantic endeavors and personal pursuits. Through his authentic self-expression, he naturally drew in individuals who valued and embraced him for his true essence.

A Tale of Fresh Starts

Daniel's foray into the dating scene following a painful breakup was a rollercoaster ride marked by triumphs and setbacks. However, it also served as a transformative period, allowing him to learn and evolve. He discovered that despite his past challenges, he gained valuable insights that helped him form healthier and more fulfilling relationships.

As you begin your adventure of starting anew after a painful experience, remember that dating presents a chance for fresh starts. Embrace it with an open heart, a desire to gain knowledge, and a dedication to remaining authentic. By approaching dating with patience, sincerity, and a positive mindset, you can confidently navigate the journey and open yourself up to the possibility of a fulfilling and significant connection.

Understanding the Contrast Between Healthy and Toxic Relationships

Once you've endured the stormy seas of heartbreak, it becomes essential to cultivate the skill of distinguishing between healthy and toxic relationships. This awareness can serve as a guiding light, allowing us to learn from our past and cultivate relationships supporting our personal growth and happiness.

The Echoes of the Past

Sophia had endured a long and exhausting relationship. Her partner's relentless criticism and manipulative actions left her feeling inadequate and bewildered. After the relationship ended, she avoided repeating the same patterns. As she re-entered the dating scene, Sophia consciously decided to pay closer attention to the indicators that differentiate a healthy relationship from a toxic one.

Signs of Trouble Ahead

During one of her initial outings following the end of her previous relationship, Sophia crossed paths with Alex. Initially, he appeared charming and attentive, but subtle warning signs soon emerged. He frequently made negative remarks about others and appeared excessively preoccupied with manipulating their intentions. Sophia observed that he seldom paid attention to her viewpoints and consistently redirected conversations toward himself.

Reminiscing about her past relationship, Sophia couldn't help but notice the familiar signs of dismissiveness and control, which had once taken a toll on her self-esteem. She followed her intuition and ended her relationship with Alex before getting too emotionally attached. For Sophia, this decision marked a significant milestone. In the past, she had faced difficulties in recognizing and responding to the warning signs of a harmful relationship.

On the other hand, Sophia quickly encountered James, who exuded a refreshing and positive aura. He showed genuine interest in getting to know her treating her with respect and kindness. James created a welcoming and appreciative atmosphere, and a shared respect and empathy characterized their exchanges.

Sophia immediately noticed the signs of a strong bond with James. He motivated her to openly communicate her thoughts and emotions, fostering a harmonious relationship where the needs of both partners were valued. James was always there to support her goals and interests, frequently offering his assistance and wanting to be a part of them. The contrast between this mutual support and respect and her previous experience is striking. In her past relationship, her partner frequently undermined her aspirations.

Exploring the Concept of Boundaries

Sophia understood the significance of setting boundaries to foster a positive and balanced relationship. Throughout her history, boundaries were frequently disregarded or brushed aside, resulting in a noticeable absence of personal space and independence. James provided a sense of security, allowing her to establish and honor boundaries. They openly discussed their comfort levels, covering personal space and communication preferences.

Take, for instance, how James acknowledged Sophia's desire for solitude, recognizing its ability to rejuvenate her. A mutual understanding of personal boundaries fostered a strong sense of security and trust between them. Sophia was empowered confident that her needs would be acknowledged and taken seriously, without any doubts or dismissals.

The Importance of Communication

Sophia noticed that effective communication was crucial in distinguishing between healthy and toxic relationships. During her past relationship, communication was frequently filled with misunderstandings and conflict. Her partner often employed manipulative tactics, like gaslighting, to undermine her perspective.

James fostered an environment of open and honest communication. They engaged in thoughtful and considerate discussions, consistently seeking to comprehend one another's perspectives. When conflicts arose, they productively handled them instead of pointing fingers or using passive-aggressive tactics. Through open and honest communication, they overcame challenges and strengthened their bond, establishing a solid base of trust and mutual understanding.

Creating a nurturing environment for emotional well-being

Sophia couldn't help but notice the strong sense of emotional safety she experienced with James. During her previous relationship, she frequently experienced feelings of anxiety and insecurity, always treading carefully to prevent setting off any negative responses. She felt alone and unappreciated due to the absence of emotional support and constant criticism.

On the other hand, James created a caring and encouraging atmosphere. He rejoiced in her achievements, provided solace during difficult moments, and consistently demonstrated understanding and compassion. Sophia found a sense of emotional security in his presence, allowing her to express herself freely without any concerns about being criticized or mocked. The foundation of their blossoming connection was the sense of emotional security, which created a space for both individuals to express their true selves without fear.

The Power of Embracing Distinctions

Sophia's experience of discovering the distinction between healthy and toxic relationships was genuinely empowering. It dawned on her that her previous encounters had imparted valuable insights into her expectations for a significant other. Sophia's newfound awareness of warning signs and focus on essential qualities such as respect, communication, and emotional support allowed her to approach her new relationships with greater discernment.

With a newfound sense of clarity, Sophia could steer clear of the mistakes she had made in the past and open herself up to healthier and more fulfilling relationships. She understood the importance of recognizing that no relationship is flawless but that a strong and positive partnership is established upon respect, understanding, and support.

Embracing a Promising Tomorrow

As Sophia ventured further into the dating world, she held onto these valuable insights. She was sure of her knack for recognizing healthy relationship dynamics and had grown unafraid of ending situations that didn't match her values. With unwavering self-assurance, she eagerly welcomed the prospect of a more promising tomorrow, envisioning a companion who would uplift and stand by her side.

Sophia's story serves as a poignant reminder of the importance of distinguishing between healthy and toxic relationships when embarking on a new chapter after experiencing heartbreak. Through a conscious awareness of the qualities that foster a harmonious and encouraging bond, individuals have the power to nurture connections that bring about happiness and personal development, ultimately leading to a future filled with love and fulfillment.

Building a Strong Connection

Establishing a Solid Foundation of Trust Over Time

Having gone through betrayal or disappointment in previous relationships, placing trust in someone new can be overwhelming. Building trust is crucial for a strong and positive connection between individuals, and restoring it requires dedication, understanding, and a willingness to work through challenges. Building trust gradually enables both individuals to establish a solid, intimate bond without feeling rushed.

Take it Step by Step.

Emma had endured a long-term relationship filled with constant betrayal and shattered trust. Her partner's deceitful behavior and refusal to be open made her feel exposed and uncertain about her worth. After the relationship ended, she committed to prioritizing trust in all her future partnerships. Emma cautiously approached her new dating experiences, being mindful not to rush into anything too quickly.

Emma and Ryan crossed paths through mutual friends, and their bond was immediate. They had a strong connection, shared interests and values, and their conversations were always captivating and full of depth. Yet, Emma understood that trust couldn't be built in a short amount of time. She opted for a more gradual approach, giving their relationship the space needed to grow organically.

Reliable Behaviour and Truthfulness

Ryan established a foundation of trust with Emma by consistently following through on his actions. He was always dependable and never failed to fulfill his commitments, whether arriving punctually for their outings or following through on their joint plans. Emma found comfort in Ryan's unwavering reliability, knowing she could always rely on him.

In addition, Ryan was transparent and sincere about his history and motives. He fearlessly addressed challenging subjects, like past relationships or personal obstacles. Because of this transparency, Emma found it easier to open up and share her own experiences and concerns. She admired Ryan's willingness to be vulnerable, which fostered an atmosphere of mutual openness and respect.

Honouring Personal Limits

Emma was cautious when establishing boundaries at the beginning of their relationship. She knew her previous encounters had made her wary and required time to develop a sense of safety. Ryan always respected her boundaries and never pushed her to go faster than she felt comfortable. He recognized the importance of establishing trust and was willing to be patient, allowing Emma the necessary space.

For example, when Emma mentioned her preference for a slower pace in their physical relationship, Ryan was incredibly supportive and understanding. He ensured her sense of security and treated her with the utmost respect, allowing her to unwind and fully savor their moments together. Acknowledging personal boundaries played a vital role in fostering their trust, demonstrating Ryan's genuine concern for Emma's comfort and welfare.

Transparent Dialogue

As Emma and Ryan's relationship developed, they consistently prioritized open communication. They had regular meetings to discuss their emotions and resolve issues or confusion. These discussions played a crucial role in establishing trust, enabling both individuals to openly and authentically express themselves without fear of criticism.

Emma was deeply moved by a specific moment. Her past relationship left her with a deep-seated fear of betrayal that still haunted her. Instead of keeping this fear to herself, she bravely chose to confide in Ryan. She recounted the painful impact of her previous partner's actions and how it occasionally triggered her anxiety. Ryan attentively listened and reassured her of his unwavering dedication to honesty and faithfulness. This conversation deepened their bond, as Emma felt genuinely listened to and empathized with.

Stories We Share

Emma and Ryan's trust was strengthened through their shared experiences. They cherished the moments they spent together, whether escaping for a weekend or simply enjoying the simple pleasures of cooking dinner or watching movies. These shared experiences strengthened their connection and provided them with new perspectives of each other.

One weekend, they embarked on a hiking adventure, which pushed Emma out of her comfort zone. Ryan, an experienced hiker, reassured her that it would be an enjoyable and secure adventure. During the hike, he showed great attentiveness and support, guiding her through the trail and providing reassurance whenever needed. This experience showcased Ryan's trustworthiness and dedication.

A Slow Unveiling

As their bond grew more pungent, Emma discovered herself opening up more and more to Ryan. She opened up about her anxieties and aspirations, and he responded kindly. Their increasing trust was evident in their mutual vulnerability. They found comfort in being their true selves with one another, confident in the acceptance and support they received.

Ryan also shared his vulnerabilities and past errors. Emma valued his sincerity and felt their bond strengthen as they explored these discussions. Their willingness to open up to one another showcased the strong bond they had formed, as it necessitated both individuals to drop their defenses and reveal their authentic selves.

Trust is an ongoing journey.

The journey of Emma and Ryan in building trust was an ongoing endeavor. They understood that trust is not a fixed endpoint but a continuous dedication. They consistently emphasized the importance of open communication, respecting boundaries, and taking consistent actions, recognizing that these factors were essential for building a solid foundation.

As time passed, Emma experienced a gradual shift in her perspective. She opened up and wholeheartedly embraced the deep love and intimacy they both cherished. She realized that her previous encounters had instilled a sense of caution but had also imparted the wisdom of approaching trust with steadiness and thoughtfulness. Emma and Ryan's relationship thrived as they patiently and consistently built trust, establishing a solid foundation for a nurturing and affectionate partnership.

This tale serves as a poignant reminder that trust when shattered, can be restored through diligent effort and unwavering patience. Through intentional actions and a natural development of trust, individuals can foster a connection built on shared respect, transparency, and emotional stability.

Developing a Deep Connection on an Emotional and Physical Level

As a new relationship develops, trust grows and paves the way for a deeper connection on both emotional and physical levels. Both elements are crucial for establishing a robust, interconnected partnership. Sharing deep thoughts and emotions strengthens the connection between partners, while physical closeness creates a special bond. Developing both necessitates a significant investment of time, a willingness to be patient, and a shared openness to vulnerability.

Building Emotional Intimacy: Exploring Inner Worlds Together

Olivia had always been cautious with her feelings, particularly after a heart-wrenching breakup that left her feeling raw and defenseless. Upon meeting Ethan, she cautiously approached, hesitating to invite him into her inner world. Nevertheless, Ethan's compassion and understanding gradually motivated her to become more vulnerable.

During the initial stages of their relationship, their discussions revolved around casual and carefree subjects. However, as time passed and their bond strengthened, their interactions took on a more profound and meaningful tone. One evening, as they relaxed on the couch with warm cups of tea, Olivia recounted a tale from her early years. She seldom spoke of it, but there was a memory that lingered in her mind—the painful divorce of her parents and the overwhelming emotional upheaval it brought upon her. Ethan was fully engaged, showing understanding and compassion without any hint of criticism.

Olivia's decision to share this story marked a turning point. She had never before opened herself up to Ethan in such a vulnerable way. His caring reaction instilled a sense of security and empathy, deepening their emotional connection. As time went on, they kept opening up to each other, sharing their deepest fears, dreams, and past experiences. With each display of vulnerability, their bond grew more assertive.

Creating a Strong Bond Through Physical Intimacy

As their connection deepened, Olivia and Ethan decided to venture into physical closeness. They both recognized the significance of this aspect of their relationship, just as they valued their emotional bond. However, considering Olivia's previous encounters, they approached it with careful consideration and respect.

Ethan was very aware of Olivia's comfort level. They began their journey with small acts of affection—holding hands, embracing, and tender caresses. These small gestures brought Olivia a sense of love and appreciation, strengthening her faith in Ethan. They had a candid conversation about their boundaries and desires, ensuring that both felt at ease and valued.

As their connection deepened, they dedicated themselves to discovering each other's preferences and boundaries. They developed a deep understanding of each other's non-verbal cues and were considerate when one required additional time or personal space. Through their thoughtful and mindful approach, they were able to develop a deep physical bond that was both secure and close.

Finding a Harmonious Blend of Emotional and Physical Connection

Olivia and Ethan constantly worked on finding a harmonious balance between their emotional and physical connection. It was found that by nurturing one aspect, the other was often enriched. After a particularly profound and heartfelt conversation, they experienced a stronger bond and a deeper connection, which naturally deepened their physical closeness.

On the other hand, their proximity frequently led to deep and meaningful discussions. During a peaceful moment of embracing, they might open up about thoughts or emotions they hadn't previously shared. The interplay between emotional and physical intimacy fostered a vibrant and ever-evolving relationship where both partners experienced a deep sense of being understood and appreciated.

Overcoming Obstacles and Personal Development

Just like any other couple, Olivia and Ethan encountered difficulties when it came to building a solid connection. Previous insecurities or fears would arise at specific points, leading to tense or misunderstood situations. Nevertheless, they saw these challenges as chances to develop. They sincerely committed to maintaining open and honest communication, handling any issues that came up with understanding and a calm demeanor.

One particular challenge arose when Olivia felt overwhelmed by the swift development of their physical closeness. She worried that Ethan may not be invested in meeting her emotional needs. Olivia openly shared her concerns with Ethan instead of keeping them to herself. He attentively listened and comforted her, expressing his deep appreciation for their emotional bond, which he cherished just as much as their physical intimacy. Through this conversation, Olivia gained a sense of reassurance and could adjust their speed, ensuring that both parties felt at ease.

Embracing the Adventure

As Olivia and Ethan continued to explore their relationship, they discovered the joy of embracing their path towards a more profound connection. They reflected on their progress, celebrating the small victories of becoming more open emotionally and the sheer joy of exploring new dimensions of physical closeness.

They also recognized that intimacy is not a final destination but a continuous journey. They were dedicated to discovering more about one another and themselves, fully embracing the vulnerabilities and joys that accompanied their journey. Their mutual patience and understanding formed the basis of a deep and affectionate relationship.

Final Thoughts: The Allure of Intimacy

The story of Olivia and Ethan showcases the intricate and captivating nature of nurturing a deep emotional connection alongside a solid physical bond. Their adventure was filled with openness, sincere dialogue, and a deep regard for one another. Through the investment of time and effort, a solid foundation of trust was established, fostering an environment where they felt secure to delve into the depths of their bond.

Their story serves as a poignant reminder that the connection between two people, in all its various manifestations, is an essential element of a thriving and satisfying partnership. It takes dedication, perseverance, and a readiness to welcome the unfamiliar. However, the benefits of forming a profound and significant bond with another individual are beyond measure for those open to embarking on this adventure.

Fostering emotional and physical closeness revolves around authentically revealing yourself to someone else and wholeheartedly accepting their true nature. It's all about building a connection where both people feel valued, encouraged, and cared for. It's all about discovering happiness in the moments we share, whether grand or minuscule, that truly make a relationship extraordinary.

Building a Strong Bond in a Fresh Partnership

Encouraging the Development of One Another

During the initial phases of a relationship, it's pretty effortless to get caught up in the thrill of discovering a new love. As the relationship progresses, it becomes essential for both partners to encourage each other's individual development. The mutual support between them strengthens their bond and cultivates a healthy and balanced partnership where both individuals can flourish.

Inspiring Aspirations and Goals

When Sarah and Michael began their relationship, they were going through periods of change. Sarah had just enrolled in school to study psychology, while Michael was considering a new career path after spending years in the corporate finance industry. They were inexplicably drawn to one another, their connection fuelled by a shared fire of passion and ambition. Their conversations naturally gravitated toward their dreams and aspirations as they eagerly shared their goals.

As the sun set and the warm ambiance of the café enveloped them, Sarah opened up about her aspirations of becoming a counselor, driven by her deep desire to support those grappling with mental health challenges. She shared her concerns and uncertainties, questioning the wisdom of altering her career trajectory at this stage of her life. Michael paid close attention to what she was saying and wholeheartedly supported her in following her passion. He emphasized her strengths and the fresh perspective she brought to the field.

Michael's unwavering support was genuinely remarkable. He was always there for Sarah, supporting her in her studies and cheering her on whenever she achieved something, no matter how big or small. Sarah provided unwavering support to Michael as he faced the challenges of his career transition. She motivated him to delve into his passion for sustainable business practices and assisted in researching potential opportunities. Through their shared support and encouragement, they developed a strong bond and a deep sense of teamwork, strengthening their dedication to each other's personal development.

Embracing Uniqueness

As their bond grew more pungent, Sarah and Michael consciously tried to preserve their unique identities. They realized the significance of fostering their identities alongside their growth as a couple. They were careful to honor one another's boundaries and interests.

Sarah had always adored painting, a passion of mine since childhood. Expressing herself and seeking solace was her chosen method. Michael greatly appreciated her talent and frequently dedicated his evenings to observing her painting. Additionally, he deeply respected her desire for solitude while she engaged in her creative process. He always respected her need for uninterrupted painting time, allowing her to immerse herself in her artfully.

Michael, however, deeply loved hiking and exploring the great outdoors. Sarah wasn't adventurous, but she wholeheartedly embraced his passion for the great outdoors. She motivated him to embark on hiking adventures with his friends and sometimes accompanied him on more accessible trails. They could strike a harmonious balance between togetherness and independence through mutual respect for their passions, resulting in a deeply fulfilling relationship.

Overcoming Adversity

Every relationship faces its fair share of challenges, and Sarah and Michael were no different. They occasionally encountered scheduling conflicts and divergent priorities as they pursued their own objectives. At times, Sarah's academic obligations would collide with Michael's longing for meaningful moments or when Michael's pursuit of employment demanded his attention be directed towards his professional aspirations rather than their relationship.

Instead of letting these challenges drive them apart, they embraced them as chances to develop and improve. They engaged in open communication, openly discussing their needs and expectations.

Sarah voiced her need for comprehension during her hectic school periods, while Michael expressed his longing for assurance as he navigated his uncertain career path.

During a particularly challenging period, Sarah faced the task of completing a demanding internship as part of her degree program. After enduring countless hours and grappling with the emotional weight of her job, she found herself drained and easily agitated. Despite feeling overlooked, Michael decided to remain patient and supportive. He embraced additional household duties and prioritized bringing happiness to their lives, such as preparing her preferred dishes or organizing a tranquil evening for them to enjoy.

Sarah, acknowledging Michael's hard work, deliberately chose to return the favor. She always made it a point to prioritize their relationship, even with her hectic schedule. Whether planning small dates or spending quality time together, she made sure they had moments to cherish. Their unwavering support for each other during difficult moments solidified their connection and enhanced their comprehension and compassion for one another.

Embracing Progress and Achievements

As Sarah and Michael continued progressing in their personal growth and relationship, they prioritized acknowledging and commemorating each other's accomplishments and significant moments. After Sarah completed her psychology degree, Michael threw a surprise party to celebrate her achievements and show his appreciation for her dedication and hard work. The atmosphere was brimming with happiness as loved ones gathered, sharing laughter and heartfelt words.

Just like that, when Michael secured a position at a sustainable business firm, Sarah wholeheartedly celebrated his accomplishment. She gifted him a personalized journal to document his new journey and accompanied him to his first day of work for moral support. These celebrations were not just about the milestones themselves but about acknowledging their journey together to reach those points.

The Importance of Mutual Growth

Sarah and Michael's relationship thrived because they viewed each other's personal growth as a shared journey. They understood that a healthy partnership involves growing together and supporting each other's individual growth. They were each other's cheerleaders, critics, and confidants, always striving to bring out the best in one another.

Their story illustrates that supporting a partner's personal growth is not just about encouraging their ambitions; it's about being present for the ups and downs, respecting their individuality, and celebrating their successes. It's about creating a partnership where people feel valued and empowered to pursue their dreams.

Ultimately, Sarah and Michael's commitment to supporting each other's growth strengthened their bond and enriched their relationship. They learned that true love is not about possessing or controlling one another but about uplifting and inspiring each other to be the best versions of themselves. This mutual support and respect laid a strong foundation for a relationship that could weather any storm and continue to grow in love and understanding.

Balancing Independence and Togetherness

One of the most delicate balancing acts in a relationship is finding the sweet spot between independence and togetherness. While sharing experiences and building a life together are essential aspects of a relationship, maintaining a sense of individuality is equally important. This balance allows both partners to grow as individuals while fostering a strong and healthy partnership.

Embracing Individual Pursuits

Lena and Jake had been dating for about a year when they moved in together. Lena and Jake both had demanding careers. Lena worked as a graphic designer, while Jake was a software developer. They relished their time together, whether it involved preparing meals, indulging in their beloved TV series, or embarking on adventures along uncharted paths. However, they also valued their hobbies and interests, essential for their personal satisfaction.

Lena had a deep passion for painting and would lose herself in her makeshift studio for hours. It served as her artistic escape and a means to relax after a hectic week. Unlike others, Jake had a deep passion for photography and often embarked on solitary journeys to capture the exquisite wonders of nature. As they embraced each other's interests, they also valued the importance of individual boundaries. Lena always enjoyed joining Jake on his photography outings, and Jake never hesitated to appreciate Lena's artwork. They supported and motivated one another to follow their passions, understanding that their individual development enhanced their bond.

Building Connections Through Shared Experiences

Lena and Jake always found time to come together and create meaningful memories, even with their hectic schedules and different passions. They recognized the significance of balancing independence with fostering their bond through meaningful moments spent together. They started having a weekly date night, quickly becoming a beloved tradition. Occasionally, they ventured to unfamiliar dining establishments, while on other occasions, they opted to stay in and prepare a meal together. These precious moments allowed them to re-establish their bond and savor each other's presence, free from work interference or personal obligations.

Traveling was a beloved pastime they both enjoyed. They relished organizing their adventures, whether it involved a brief escape to a neighboring town or an extended journey to a foreign land. These exciting escapades offered them fresh encounters and deepened their connection. They discovered the art of exploring unknown territories side by side, tackling challenges as a united front, and embracing the wonders of immersing themselves in different cultures. These collective experiences forged enduring memories and fostered a more profound comprehension of one another.

Exploring the Complexities of Conflicts and Compromises

Achieving the perfect equilibrium between individuality and unity had its fair share of challenges. At specific points, their personal goals conflicted with their longing for quality time as a group. During a particular time, Lena faced a significant project deadline demanding that she work late at night and on weekends. Sensing a lack of attention, Jake organized a weekend getaway to re-establish a connection. They reached a point where Lena had to prioritize her work while Jake longed for more meaningful moments together.

Instead of letting this cause conflict, they openly discussed their needs. Lena empathized with Jake's emotions and proposed they organize a vacation after finishing her project. Jake recognized the significance of Lena's work and consented to be patient. They found small moments to bond amidst the hustle and bustle, such as sharing breakfast or strolls in the evening. By finding a compromise, they could balance their individual responsibilities and stay connected.

Honouring Personal Limits

Respecting each other's boundaries is another important aspect of balancing independence and togetherness. Lena and Jake respected each other's boundaries, ensuring they didn't invade their personal space. They established firm limits regarding personal time, recognizing its importance for rejuvenation and introspection.

As an avid photographer, Jake cherished Sunday mornings as a precious opportunity to immerse himself in editing photos and mapping out his upcoming projects. Lena appreciated this and utilized that time to engage in her activities, such as practicing yoga or indulging in a good book. Like that, Lena enjoyed dedicating some of her weekends to attending workshops at a nearby art studio. Jake was always there to support and encourage her in pursuing these opportunities, fully aware of the immense happiness they brought her. Thanks to their mutual understanding of boundaries, they could appreciate their pursuits without any negative emotions.

The Advantages of Finding Balance

Lena and Jake discovered that their relationship was a perfect blend of independence and togetherness, resulting in a fulfilling and dynamic connection. They were both allowed to pursue their passions and discover new things, which brought excitement and vitality to their relationship. Simultaneously, they treasured the moments they spent together, building a solid base of trust and mutual respect.

Their ability to maintain this equilibrium also allowed them to handle obstacles more effortlessly. They possessed a profound comprehension of one another's needs and priorities, reducing conflicts and misunderstandings. They discovered that a strong relationship thrives not on constant togetherness but on a balanced mix of shared and individual experiences.

Final Thoughts: A Beautiful Synchronisation

Lena and Jake's story beautifully captures the delicate dance of maintaining individuality while nurturing a deep connection within a relationship. It's a beautiful symphony that requires honest dialogue, shared admiration, and a readiness to find a middle ground. They fully embraced their unique qualities, wholeheartedly pursued their interests, and always prioritized their connection, forming an incredibly fulfilling and encouraging partnership.

They were able to strike a perfect balance, allowing them to thrive individually and as a couple. Their relationship flourished with vibrancy and a zest for life. It served as a reminder that genuine love is not about sacrificing one's identity for another but discovering happiness in individual independence and mutual bonds. Amidst this delicate equilibrium, they unearthed a profound and all-encompassing love that honored their unique identities while cherishing their unity.

PART 5
Embracing A Resilient Love

EMBRACING A RESILIENT LOVE

Embrace the strength of resilient love—by handling challenges with understanding, celebrating shared growth, and nurturing lasting passion, you cultivate a love that thrives through every season of life

Handling Challenges in New Relationships

Addressing Conflicts Constructively

Conflicts are bound to arise in any relationship. Issues can emerge from miscommunications, varying assumptions, or just the everyday pressures of life. Nevertheless, building a solid and enduring relationship requires us to confront conflicts positively and constructively. This method encourages comprehension, enhances individual connection, and supports development.

A Glimpse into the Beginning of Turmoil

Sarah and Alex had been dating for a few months when they encountered their first significant disagreement. It all began with a seemingly insignificant dispute: how to spend their weekend. Sarah enjoyed a peaceful evening at home, indulging in films and unwinding, while Alex was excited to venture out and discover the city. A seemingly innocuous disagreement soon turned into a fiery dispute. Both individuals experienced a sense of being ignored and growing frustration, ultimately resulting in hurt emotions for both parties involved.

Amidst the situation's intensity, they both were caught in unproductive patterns. Feeling hurt by Alex's apparent disregard for her need for rest, Sarah withdrew into herself. Meanwhile, Alex, sensing that Sarah was dismissing his longing for adventure, became defensive. This initial clash had the potential to create a divide between them, but instead, it turned into a crucial moment in their relationship.

Reflecting on the Situation

After calming down, Sarah and Alex realized they should approach their conflict more carefully. They chose to have a candid conversation about the events that had transpired. This conversation signaled the start of their path toward positive conflict resolution.

They began by recognizing each other's emotions. Sarah mentioned feeling overwhelmed by the hectic week and wanted some much-needed relaxation. Alex expressed his excitement about exploring new experiences together but felt let down by the lack of enthusiasm from the other person. Through actively listening to one another refraining from interruptions or defensiveness, they gradually gained insight into the underlying cause of their disagreement.

Discovering Shared Perspectives

After better grasping one another's viewpoints, Sarah and Alex collaborated to reach a middle ground. They realized that the matter was not about assigning blame or determining who was right or wrong but rather about finding a way to harmonize their individual needs. They reached an agreement to take turns on weekends—one for staying in and the other for going out. They accommodated Sarah's need for rest while satisfying Alex's desire for exploration.

During this journey, they realized the significance of adaptability and understanding when resolving conflicts. Instead of stubbornly holding onto their preferences, they discovered the worth of each other's desires. Their ability to find common ground became a fundamental aspect of their relationship, enabling them to handle future conflicts more smoothly.

Mastering the Art of Effective Communication

As Sarah and Alex continued their relationship, they made it a priority to enhance their communication abilities. They recognized the importance of open and considerate communication in effectively addressing conflicts. They deliberately chose to communicate their emotions and desires without resorting to accusations or disapproval. Sarah found that expressing her feelings of being unheard when her needs weren't considered was more effective than accusing the other person of never listening. This language change allowed them to address their issues without causing further tension.

In addition, they made a point of actively listening to one another, fully grasping each other's concerns before responding. They made sure to give their complete focus, asking for clarification when needed and repeating what they heard to ensure comprehension. Through this approach, they were able to reduce any potential confusion and cultivate a stronger emotional bond.

The Importance of Timing and Space

Sarah and Alex discovered another crucial element of effective conflict resolution: the significance of timing and personal boundaries. They understood that attempting to address disagreements when emotions were still intense often resulted in unproductive discussions. Instead, they decided to pause and return to the matter when they were both more composed. By adopting this approach, they tackled conflicts with a more focused mindset and a stronger determination to seek resolutions.

A Tale of Growth and Resilience

As time passed, Sarah and Alex realized that dealing with and resolving conflicts positively improved their relationship. Every disagreement presented a chance to gain a deeper understanding of one another and to develop both as individuals and as a couple. They grew more skilled at navigating their differences, cultivating a more profound comprehension of each other's values, boundaries, and emotional triggers.

Alex faced a particularly challenging situation when they had to relocate to a new city for work. Both were filled with fears and insecurities when they considered the idea of a long-distance relationship. Instead of allowing these emotions to simmer, they confronted them directly. They openly discussed their concerns, devised plans for regular visits, and brainstormed strategies to sustain their connection despite the geographical separation. By taking a proactive approach, they successfully navigated the transition and strengthened their bond.

Embracing the Power of Enduring Love

The journey of Sarah and Alex showcases how conflicts, when approached with a constructive mindset, can foster growth and resilience within a relationship. They could navigate their differences with grace and understanding by focusing on open communication, empathy, and flexibility. They fully embraced that conflicts are not a sign of a failing relationship but rather an opportunity to strengthen their bond.

Sarah and Alex's journey taught them that true love is not defined by the absence of obstacles but by the strength and commitment to confront them side by side. They developed a partnership where both individuals felt appreciated, listened to, and treated with respect, enabling them to establish a solid basis for a long-lasting and satisfying relationship. Their tale is a powerful reminder that by adopting a positive mindset and utilizing the appropriate resources, any couple can turn conflicts into valuable chances for personal development and deepening their bond.

The Significance of Finding Common Ground and Empathy

Maya and Sam were utterly inseparable during the early stages of their relationship. Their bond was powerful, and they had many shared interests and values. Nevertheless, as they ventured through the intricacies of their collaboration, they started to come across disparities that challenged their connection. There were various distinctions between them, from their choices for weekend activities to their money management methods. It quickly became evident that their willingness to find common ground and empathize with each other would be essential in preserving a peaceful relationship.

A Weekend Conundrum

One ongoing issue revolved around their weekend preferences. Maya, a lover of solitude, treasured peaceful weekends at home, immersing herself in books and culinary pursuits. Sam, however, was quite the social butterfly, always seeking out social activities and enjoying the company of friends. Their conflicting preferences frequently caused tension and misunderstandings, making weekends a potential breeding ground for conflict.

Initially, both individuals tried to please each other by putting aside their wants. Maya reluctantly agreed to attend social gatherings, while Sam spent weekends at home, feeling restless. Unfortunately, this method left both individuals feeling unsatisfied and aggravated. They realized that relinquishing their preferences alone would not be a viable long-term solution.

A Lesson in Compromise

It was pivotal when Maya and Sam opened up to each other, discussing their desires and emotions. They recognized that their divergences were not impassable barriers but give-and-take opportunities. They agreed to alternate selecting their weekend activities. On weekends, their routine alternated between peaceful days at home and lively outings with friends.

Through this arrangement, they could acknowledge and fulfill each other's needs while valuing their own. Maya realized the importance of balancing social outings and quiet weekends, while Sam found happiness in spending peaceful days with Maya. This resolution solved their weekend predicament and strengthened their mutual comprehension.

Exploring Financial Decisions and Enhancing Understanding

Maya and Sam encountered difficulties when it came to handling their finances. Maya was known for her careful nature, always thinking ahead and planning for the future. In contrast, Sam had a more carefree and spontaneous attitude, embracing the present moment and finding joy in it. These variations resulted in conflicts regarding expenditures and savings, especially when organizing trips or buying expensive items.

Instead of letting their financial differences create a divide, Maya and Sam confronted the issue directly. They settled in and had a conversation about their economic aspirations and worries. Maya voiced her concern about her lack of savings for unexpected situations, while Sam expressed his longing to fully embrace and enjoy life's experiences in the present moment.

They could come to a shared understanding by engaging in an open conversation. They crafted a budget that perfectly balanced their financial goals: a portion of their income was dedicated to building savings and making investments. In contrast, another portion was reserved for enjoying discretionary spending and memorable experiences. They could effectively handle their finances without any lingering resentment by reaching a compromise. It was a situation where both of their viewpoints were acknowledged and taken into account.

Developing a Deeper Understanding and Practicing Tolerance

As Maya and Sam encountered different obstacles, they understood that finding common ground involved more than just finding practical answers. It also meant showing understanding and being patient. They discovered the art of understanding different viewpoints and valuing the motivations behind their partner's choices and actions.

Maya realized that Sam's interest in social activities wasn't a way of pushing her away but rather a way for him to fulfill his need for social interaction. Sam understood that Maya's tendency to save was not a sign of being unspontaneous but rather a way for her to prioritize stability and security.

Through the practice of empathy, they adopted a compassionate and understanding approach when faced with disagreements. They discovered how to effectively express their needs without assigning blame and developed the ability to truly listen to one another without passing judgment. It fostered an environment where individuals felt comfortable sharing their thoughts and positively resolving conflicts.

The Importance of Adaptability

Being open to compromise necessitates a certain level of flexibility. Maya and Sam realized that being inflexible with their preferences could result in deadlocks and hard feelings. Instead, they adopted a mindset of adaptability, enabling them to adjust to shifting circumstances and the evolving needs of one another.

When Sam experienced a particularly demanding week at work, Maya proposed that they forgo their usual social outing and instead enjoy a peaceful evening at home. Just like that, when Maya mentioned her longing to explore new places, Sam readily agreed to prioritize saving for a vacation. Their dedication to one another's happiness and well-being was evident in their willingness to be flexible.

Building the Bedrock of Enduring Affection

Maya and Sam's journey showcases the significance of compromise and understanding in cultivating a solid and enduring love. Their mutual understanding, ability to see things from each other's point of view, and willingness to adapt formed the basis of a solid and enduring relationship. They realized that genuine collaboration is not about triumphing or failing but about collaborating to build a life that respects the needs and desires of both individuals.

Maya and Sam discovered that finding common ground is not a display of vulnerability but rather a demonstration of resilience that cultivates a sense of mutual admiration and reliance. Open communication, empathy, and a sincere desire to support each other's growth and happiness are essential. Their tale is a powerful testament to the transformative power of a positive outlook and approach. It reminds us that even in the face of challenges, we can forge stronger bonds and gain a deeper understanding, ultimately leading to resilient and everlasting love.

Crafting a Collective Vision for the Future

Establishing Shared Objectives and Ambitions

During the initial stages of their relationship, Emma and Daniel reveled in impromptu escapades and fully embraced the present. As their bond grew more robust, they realized the significance of making joint plans for the future. They realized that having a shared vision for their lives would deepen their connection and give them a clear path to follow as a couple.

Let the Story Unfold

Emma and Daniel had been dating for over a year, and they finally discussed their future together. The conversation started in a relaxed manner during dinner, as Emma enquired about Daniel's aspirations for the future. Daniel spoke about his dream of starting a family and creating a secure and loving home, while Emma talked about her ambitions to progress in her career and explore different parts of the world. They both realized that their personal goals held significance, but they also had to consider how these ambitions aligned with their life together.

From that point on, a cascade of profound conversations unfolded, delving into their core beliefs, aspirations, and vision for their future. They realized the importance of sharing common goals to create a future that would fulfill their desires.

Discovering Shared Territory

Emma and Daniel began by pinpointing their fundamental values and priorities. Both cherished the importance of family, stability, and adventure, yet they held contrasting perspectives on attaining these aspirations. Daniel envisioned a suburban home where he could focus on raising children. On the other hand, Emma imagined living in a bustling city, fully immersed in her career and enjoying frequent travels.

Instead of viewing these differences as challenges, they saw them as chances to discover shared interests. They explored different possibilities and agreements that would enable them to harmonize their aspirations. Emma recommended considering job opportunities in a city that provides career prospects and cultural experiences, while Daniel suggested prioritizing regular family vacations to fulfill their travel aspirations.

Crafting a Vision Board

Emma and Daniel joined forces to bring their shared vision to life by creating a vision board. They gathered a collection of images, quotes, and symbols that symbolized their aspirations and ambitions. The vision board showcased a collection of captivating visuals, ranging from their ideal abode to breathtaking destinations they yearned to explore, along with symbolic depictions of their ambitious career goals.

This visual depiction of their future constantly reminded them of their common goals. In addition, it offered a means to monitor their advancement and commemorate significant achievements throughout their journey. With every new addition to the board, their dedication and anticipation for their future grew stronger.

Establishing Shared Objectives

Emma and Daniel used their vision board as inspiration to establish specific goals together. They set up some immediate objectives, like saving up for a vacation and locating a city that provided job prospects and a family-friendly atmosphere. In addition, they established ambitious long-term goals, such as purchasing a house and beginning a family.

A timeline was established for these goals, dividing them into achievable steps. As an illustration, their plan involved researching cities in the upcoming six months to relocate within a year. They established financial goals for their vacation savings and started exploring residential areas suitable for families.

Encouraging and uplifting one another's dreams and goals.

Emma and Daniel recognized the importance of working together and encouraging each other's ambitions to achieve their shared objectives. Emma persisted in her pursuit of her career aspirations, fuelled by Daniel's unwavering support. Meanwhile, Daniel diligently worked to establish a secure and comfortable home while uplifting Emma professionally.

They deliberately honored and commemorated each other's achievements and significant moments. After Emma received a promotion, Daniel decided to organize a special dinner to celebrate her accomplishment. Just like that, when Daniel finished an important project at work, Emma planned a delightful weekend escape. Their actions were a powerful reminder of their unwavering dedication to each other's aspirations as they pursued their collective goal.

Overcoming Obstacles Together

Emma and Daniel faced various obstacles and setbacks as they pursued their objectives. They encountered unforeseen obstacles in their job hunts, financial strains, and conflicting viewpoints on specific choices. Instead of allowing these challenges to create distance, they saw them as opportunities to enhance their partnership.

When conflicts arose, they returned to their shared vision board and goals. They reflected on their mutual aspirations and the factors that brought them together. They could maintain their practice by staying focused on their long-term vision and having a framework for resolving conflicts.

Reflecting on Accomplishments

Emma and Daniel made sure to commemorate their achievements along their journey, taking the opportunity to acknowledge their progress. They recognized and rejoiced in every accomplishment, whether it was a successful relocation to their desired city, a cherished family trip, or completing a significant project.

These festivities solidified their common goal and deepened their connection. They discovered that the path to their aspirations held just as much significance as reaching their final destination, and commemorating their team accomplishments strengthened their bond.

A Future We Share

Emma and Daniel's story highlights the significance of establishing a shared vision for the future in a relationship. Through establishing shared objectives, exploring shared interests, and unwavering support of each other's dreams, they forged a solid basis for their shared journey. Their steadfast dedication to pursuing their aspirations and commemorating their achievements enabled them to overcome obstacles and strengthen their bond.

This tale serves as a poignant reminder that a love that endures is forged through a mutual vision and a steadfast dedication to pursuing it hand in hand. Couples can forge a path towards a future that harmoniously blends their personal aspirations and joint ambitions through a shared vision and mutual encouragement.

Celebrating Milestones and Growth Together

With the shifting of the seasons, the milestones in Lily and Max's relationship also transformed. As they rejoiced in their little triumphs and significant milestones, their joint dream of a meaningful life together started to materialize. Every considerable moment, whether an individual achievement or a shared experience, was a powerful reminder of their unwavering dedication and deep affection.

First Milestone: Moving In Together

One of their earliest significant achievements was when they decided to live under the same roof. Lily and Max had spent numerous evenings discussing their perfect living situation, settling on a comfortable flat that perfectly combined their need for coziness and convenience. On the day they arrived, the air was filled with anticipation. Hours were dedicated to unpacking boxes, arranging furniture, and envisioning their future in the new space.

As the sun set, they settled onto their freshly arranged couch, surrounded by a sea of unopened boxes. They enjoyed a humble meal of takeaway pizza, savoring the moment together. During all the commotion of relocating, they were determined to commemorate the event. They raised their glasses to celebrate their new home and the promising days ahead, reminiscing about the path that led them to this moment. The celebration focused on recognizing the importance of their collective accomplishment rather than extravagant displays.

Second Milestone: Advancing in Your Career

After several months, Lily and Max reached essential milestones in their careers. Lily achieved a significant milestone in her professional journey as she was promoted to a managerial position at her company. Meanwhile, Max experienced a pivotal moment in his career when he successfully secured a significant project at work. These accomplishments were not just individual triumphs but reflected their shared support and motivation.

They were excited and excited as they planned a weekend escape to a charming town nearby. They spent their days hiking, discovering local attractions, and savoring peaceful dinners at delightful restaurants. This journey went beyond being a mere getaway; it became a commemoration of their relentless efforts, their unwavering commitment to one another, and the personal and relational development they underwent. They took the opportunity to reflect on their journey, express gratitude for their accomplishments, and discuss their future goals.

Third Milestone: Celebrating Anniversaries and Reflecting on Personal Growth

Anniversaries became a cherished occasion for looking back on their journey and rejoicing in their love as their bond deepened. Lily and Max decided to take a trip down memory lane on their first anniversary. They looked back at the vision board they had made together, filled with dreams and aspirations for their future. They added new goals and dreams, highlighting the progress they had achieved and the fresh aspirations they had formed.

Their anniversary dinner was a significant event. They returned to their beloved restaurant and reflected on their shared journey. They expressed their aspirations and ambitions for the upcoming year, commemorating their affection and the personal development they had undergone. They gave each other meaningful presents representing their mutual adventure and dedication to encouraging one another's dreams.

Fourth Milestone: Overcoming Challenges as a Team

Like it always does, life brought forth its fair share of obstacles. Lily and Max encountered unexpected challenges, including major home repairs and unforeseen financial burdens. Despite their obstacles, they consciously confronted them as a team, refusing to let them diminish their accomplishments.

They tackled every obstacle together, using their collective creativity to find solutions and offering unwavering support during times of stress and uncertainty. Every obstacle presented itself as a chance to strengthen their dedication and perseverance. They rejoiced in their triumph over challenges, seeing these instances as markers of their resilience and solidarity.

The Importance of Celebrating in Cultivating a Strong and Lasting Love

Throughout their journey, Lily and Max discovered the importance of acknowledging and commemorating their accomplishments, regardless of their magnitude. Celebrations were more than just a way to recognize their achievements; they reminded them of their shared goals and the strong bond that united them. Every celebration deepened their bond, constantly reminding them of their intertwined path and their unwavering dedication to constructing a future side by side.

They realized that commemorating significant moments allowed them to take a break, acknowledge their progress, and recommit to one another. During these moments of joy and reflection, they discovered a wellspring of strength, motivation, and a profound sense of connection.

A Relationship Forged Through Joint Victories

Lily and Max's story beautifully emphasizes the significance of commemorating milestones and personal development within a relationship. Recognizing and celebrating their accomplishments strengthened their shared vision and forged a stronger connection. Every celebration showcased their unwavering strength, dedication, and affection.

Their story is a testament to the power of enduring love, which is strengthened by conquering obstacles and cherishing the triumphs that come their way. Couples can establish a solid base of mutual happiness and harmony by acknowledging their achievements and contemplating their personal development, setting the stage for meaningful and lasting love.

Fostering enduring love and happiness

Keeping the Flame Alive: Nurturing Passion and Romance

Amidst the fast-paced cadence of daily existence, it is often effortless to allow enthusiasm and love to fade into the background. However, keeping the flame alive in their long-term relationship became a top concern for Mia and Ethan. As they established their daily rhythm, they understood that maintaining the enchantment demanded purpose and dedication. They realized that a relationship cannot flourish solely on love; it requires ongoing care and imagination.

The Daily Routines

Mia and Ethan discovered immense happiness in establishing simple, everyday traditions that nurtured their bond and kept it alive. Every morning, before starting their day, they made it a habit to enjoy a peaceful cup of coffee in each other's company. These quiet moments allowed them to bond before the hustle and bustle of the day consumed their attention. During this period, they took the opportunity to discuss their plans and show gratitude and affection towards one another. This simple ritual became a beloved part of their everyday routine, a constant reminder of their deep affection amid life's tumultuousness.

A Fresh Take on Date Nights

Evening outings, previously a monthly highlight, became more impromptu and imaginative. Mia and Ethan consciously decided to dedicate one evening to a particular date night every week but with a unique twist. They would alternate in organizing these evenings, each striving to delight the other with one-of-a-kind adventures. Their date nights were filled with endless possibilities for creativity and fun, whether cooking a meal from a new cuisine or organizing a themed movie marathon.

One unforgettable evening, Ethan pleasantly surprised Mia with a delightful stargazing picnic. He created a warm and inviting atmosphere in their backyard with the addition of twinkling lights and a telescope. As they lay side by side beneath the sparkling night sky, they lost themselves in a sea of cherished moments and hopeful aspirations. This considerate act reignited their spirit of exploration and served as a gentle reminder of the significance of love and passion.

Keeping the Flame Burning by Cultivating Common Hobbies

Mia and Ethan consciously tried to explore common hobbies and activities, which helped strengthen their bond. They stumbled upon a shared passion for dancing and enrolled in salsa classes as a duo. Attending the classes offered a delightful opportunity for them to connect on a deeper level while venturing into a fresh pastime and pushing their limits as a duo. They discovered immense happiness through their journey of learning and evolving as a unit, and the moments they shared on the dance floor fostered a profound bond that extended far beyond their time spent dancing.

Exploring the Complexities of Intimacy

Mia and Ethan encountered their fair share of obstacles, like any other relationship. Amidst their challenges, they understood the importance of nurturing their connection to stay strong. They were determined to be transparent and honest in communicating their emotions and worries. Through shared experiences and a deep sense of compassion, they discovered the power of facing challenges as a united front, preserving their love amidst adversity.

A significant challenge arose when Ethan was promoted to a highly demanding position at work. This new role demanded longer hours and increased levels of stress. Mia shouldered additional responsibilities at home and organizing weekend getaways to help him rejuvenate. During these breaks, they found solace in each other's company, using the time to strengthen their connection and renew their dedication. Rather than allowing stressful moments to drive them apart, they saw them as chances to grow closer.

Reflecting on Accomplishments and Reaching New Heights

Mia and Ethan found joy in commemorating their accomplishments and significant moments, which helped them maintain their enthusiasm. They were committed to acknowledging and celebrating achievements, no matter their significance or insignificance. No matter the occasion, they always commemorate it as a team.

They decided to celebrate their fifth anniversary by organizing a spontaneous getaway to a city that had always been on their travel bucket list. The journey was brimming with adventure, joy, and instances of contemplation on their shared path. Marking these significant achievements made them value their progress and strengthen their collective objectives.

The Impact of Considerate Actions

Mia and Ethan knew the significance of considerate actions in sustaining their love. Leaving little notes for each other became a regular practice, a way to express their emotions and gratitude. These notes, cleverly tucked away in surprising spots such as a briefcase or a cherished book, acted as gentle daily reminders of their deep affection.

They would delight one another during special moments with heartfelt presents or memorable adventures. Ethan lovingly presented Mia with a scrapbook brimming with cherished memories from their time together, while Mia delighted Ethan with a spontaneous weekend escape to his beloved fishing spot. These small gestures were instrumental in keeping their passion alive.

The Adventure Goes On

Mia and Ethan found themselves on a continuous journey to maintain passion and romance as they navigated the ups and downs of their relationship. It took a lot of imagination, hard work, and a solid dedication to one another. Through their daily rituals, spontaneous date nights, shared interests, and thoughtful gestures, they cultivated a deep connection that endured and flourished.

Their account emphasizes the importance of consistently nurturing a relationship to maintain vitality. Through commemorating significant achievements, facing obstacles as a team, and cherishing life's simple pleasures, couples can promote a love that withstands the test of time and grows stronger. Mia and Ethan's journey is a beautiful testament to the enduring power of love. It reminds us that true romance requires constant care and dedication to cultivate and preserve their deep connection.

Embracing the Power of Gratitude and Appreciation

At the core of their relationship, Olivia and Alex stumbled upon a profound revelation for nurturing their love: cultivating gratitude and appreciation. Although their affection for one another had always been strong, they came to value the depth of their connection and the ordinary moments they experienced together through purposeful displays of appreciation.

A Daily Gratitude Ritual

Olivia and Alex embarked on a humble yet life-changing tradition. Every evening, as they prepared to sleep, they made it a habit to reflect on what they appreciated about one another and their bond. They discovered a serene moment, devoid of disturbances, to exchange their thoughts.

Amidst the chaos of the day, Olivia expresses her gratitude for your handling of a challenging situation at work. It was comforting to see how calm and patient you were. Your actions made me feel more secure. Alex expressed gratitude for how you took care of dinner tonight, especially after a long day. I truly appreciate your constant consideration for us. It holds great significance to me.

These moments of gratitude became a beloved part of their nightly routine. They discovered that showing gratitude deepened their bond and made it easier for them to handle the difficulties of everyday life. It served as a poignant reminder that no matter how challenging or overwhelming the circumstances, there were always countless reasons to express gratitude for one another.

Embracing the Beauty of Small Acts of Kindness

Olivia and Alex were sure to acknowledge and celebrate small acts of kindness. One evening, Alex delighted Olivia with her favorite dessert, which he had meticulously crafted. Olivia didn't just assume it, and she showed her appreciation with a sincere note. She placed the note gently on Alex's pillow, ensuring he would discover it before retiring for the night.

Upon reading the note, gratitude washed over me for the unexpected delight that graced my evening. These small gestures remind me of my immense gratitude for your presence in my life. Alex's smile when he read the note spoke volumes about the impact of these small gestures of appreciation. It was clear that your thoughtfulness meant a lot to him.

The Impact of Considerate Actions

They also realized the impact of considerate actions in strengthening their appreciation. During significant moments like their anniversary, they craft unique presents honoring their shared experiences. Olivia put together a beautiful scrapbook for their third anniversary, filled with cherished photos, meaningful mementos, and heartfelt handwritten notes that captured their special moments together. Alex received a personalized painting that depicted a special moment they shared at a particular location, preserving a treasured memory.

These considerate actions were more than just about exchanging presents, but rather about expressing the significance they placed on one another's company and the moments they had shared. Creating something meaningful became a beautiful way for them to express their profound appreciation and love.

Appreciating and Esteeming Hard Work

Olivia and Alex discovered the significance of acknowledging and appreciating one another's contributions. They always recognized and appreciated each other's efforts in building their life together. They ensured that their efforts, whether taking on extra responsibilities at home or planning a special date night, were not overlooked.

After a grueling week of late nights at work, Alex was pleasantly surprised when Olivia planned a rejuvenating weekend escape for the two of them. When Alex expressed his appreciation, he said, "I'm grateful for you organizing this trip." It serves as a reminder of Olivia's gratitude towards her partner, who always prioritizes her well-being. Her smile in response reflects her deep appreciation for his sincere words.

Transforming Difficulties into Favourable Circumstances

Practicing gratitude played a significant role in helping Olivia and Alex transform their challenges into valuable opportunities for personal growth. When confronted with disagreements or challenging circumstances, they would take a moment to contemplate what they appreciated about one another. By shifting their perspective, they could approach conflicts with a more profound sense of empathy and understanding.

Amidst a particularly intense phase, Olivia discovered herself growing increasingly exasperated with certain behaviors exhibited by Alex. Instead of dwelling on the downsides, she consciously remembered the positive attributes she appreciated about him. She recounted her thoughts to Alex, who reciprocated with his appreciation for her understanding and encouragement. By adopting this approach, they could tackle their problems with a fresh perspective and more tremendous admiration.

A Timeless Testament of Affection

As Olivia and Alex embarked on practicing gratitude and appreciation, they created a beautiful legacy filled with love and happiness that would endure for years to come. They realized that these practices went beyond improving their relationship and instead focused on strengthening their bond and bringing more joy into their lives.

Their tale emphasises the importance of nurturing a lasting love, which goes beyond mere effort. It calls for a sincere admiration for one another and the life they create as a team. Through daily gratitude, the celebration of small acts of kindness, the acknowledgement of each other's efforts, and the ability to transform challenges into opportunities, couples can cultivate a resilient and profoundly fulfilling love.

The experience of Olivia and Alex is a powerful reminder of how love can thrive when nurtured with appreciation and gratitude. Their story highlights the significance of cherishing ordinary moments, commemorating accomplishments, and acknowledging the dedication required to create a lasting and affectionate relationship.

CONCLUSION

As we come to the end of our exploration into love, healing, and new beginnings, it is essential to take a moment and contemplate the journey we have embarked upon. Finding love after heartbreak is a journey that doesn't follow a straight path. It's a meandering road that is marked by moments of self-reflection, personal development, and rejuvenation. This journey is a profoundly personal experience that resonates with anyone who longs to rebuild and rediscover the profound connection that love can bring.

Embracing Your Progress and Recovery

Recognizing progress involves taking a moment to appreciate growth and healing. Consider the transformations that have taken place within you—how you have come to accept vulnerability, how you have evolved from previous relationships, and how you have restored your sense of self-value. These achievements, even if they may appear insignificant at the time, are essential in your journey. They serve as evidence of your unwavering determination and ability to overcome challenges.

Pause and acknowledge the time and energy you've dedicated to gaining a deeper understanding of yourself, cultivating self-compassion, and getting ready for what lies ahead. Embrace the bravery required to face your history, the knowledge acquired from those moments, and the optimism you have nurtured for what lies ahead. Regardless of how cautious, every small progress made is an achievement that should be recognized and celebrated.

Recognizing the Ongoing Process of Healing

Healing is a continuous journey rather than a fixed endpoint. It's essential to recognize that although there has been progress, the path of healing and personal development is ongoing. There may be moments of difficulty and occasions when past hurts resurface, but these are not setbacks—they are integral to the continuing journey of personal growth and healing.

Embrace the ongoing process of healing with a compassionate and patient mindset. It is expected to experience moments of uncertainty or sadness; these emotions are natural parts of the healing process. Recognizing that healing is an ongoing process allows you to embrace growth and change, enabling you to stay receptive to the endless opportunities that life and love present.

Embracing a Bright Future

As we gaze into the future, holding onto a positive outlook is crucial. The future is full of exciting opportunities for love and connection, and your past experiences have equipped you with a greater self-awareness and a better understanding of what you truly desire. Hope is a potent energy that propels us towards our dreams and motivates us to pursue the love and joy we are worthy of.

As you journey ahead, may hope to illuminate your path. Imagine the connections you desire to form and the future you aspire to shape. Embrace the idea that you deserve love and have the ability to create meaningful relationships. Embracing a positive outlook will draw in favorable experiences and strengthen your dedication to fostering and maintaining the love you desire.

Exploring the Boundless Potential of Love and Connection

Love and connection offer a multitude of possibilities, each unique and diverse. Every fresh connection brings the possibility of happiness, personal development, and shared understanding. Embrace these opportunities with a sense of adventure and a genuine desire to discover more profound levels of closeness and understanding.

Embrace new connections with the wisdom you've gained and the strength you've developed. Have faith in building relationships rooted in mutual respect, shared values, and sincere fondness. By remaining receptive to the endless possibilities, you pave the way for meaningful and enduring relationships to thrive.

The Strength of Perseverance and an Optimistic Perspective

Having a solid sense of resilience and maintaining a positive outlook can significantly impact one's experience in the realm of love. How you've overcome previous heartbreaks and approach new experiences with optimism truly showcases your inner resilience. This strength enables you to confront challenges with bravery and to see setbacks as chances for personal development instead of barriers.

Developing a positive perspective involves directing your attention toward the positive aspects of your life and reflecting on the valuable lessons gained from your past encounters. By embracing a positive outlook, you can strengthen your capacity to attract and cultivate meaningful connections, allowing you to stay receptive to life's wonders and possibilities.

Closing Reflections and Words of Encouragement

As we wrap up this exploration of love and healing, it's essential to remember that your journey is entirely individual and personal. Celebrate your progress and keep acknowledging the growth that accompanies every step. Your experiences have molded you into someone capable of experiencing deep love and forming meaningful connections with others.

Take care of yourself as you navigate the intricacies of relationships, and keep pursuing the happiness and satisfaction you are worthy of. Love, in all its various manifestations, possesses an incredible strength that can bestow profound joy and facilitate personal development. Have faith in the adventure confidence in your value, and stay receptive to the affection ahead.

Inspiring a Journey of Personal Exploration

Love and self-discovery go hand in hand. Keep delving into your inner world, uncovering more about yourself, what you long for, and what you require. Exploring one's true self is an ongoing journey that enhances one's capacity to form genuine connections and cultivate meaningful bonds with others. Embark on this adventure with a sense of wonder and receptiveness, allowing it to lead you to more profound and gratifying relationships.

A Story of Hope for All Those in Search of Love

To all those searching for love after experiencing heartbreak, your journey is a testament to your bravery, strength, and optimism. The journey ahead is not without obstacles, yet it presents countless chances for personal development, happiness, and meaningful relationships. Have faith in your capacity to heal, evolve, and welcome the love waiting for you.

May your journey be guided by the joy of self-exploration and the embrace of fresh starts. Always remember that love is not merely a final destination but a continuous journey. And rest assured, you possess the ability to navigate this journey with elegance and optimism. Embrace the endless possibilities that await you with an open heart, and may your journey guide you toward the love and happiness you truly deserve.

www.ingramcontent.com/pod-product-compliance
Lightning Source LLC
Chambersburg PA
CBHW040830010826
48978CB00012BB/683